HARLEQUIN®
Presents~

In Harlequin Presents books seduction and passion are
always guaranteed, and this month is no exception!
You'll love what we have to offer you this April....

Favorite author Helen Bianchin brings us
The Marriage Possession, where a devilishly
handsome millionaire demands his pregnant
mistress marry him. In part two of Sharon Kendrick's
enticingly exotic THE DESERT PRINCES trilogy,
The Sheikh's Unwilling Wife, the son of a powerful
desert ruler is determined to make his estranged wife
resume her position by his side.

If you love passionate Mediterranean men, then these
books will definitely be ones to look out for! In
Lynne Graham's *The Italian's Inexperienced Mistress,*
an Italian tycoon finds that one night with an innocent
English girl just isn't enough! Then in Kate Walker's
Sicilian Husband, Blackmailed Bride, a sinfully
gorgeous Sicilian vows to reclaim his wife in his bed.
In *At the Greek Boss's Bidding,* Jane Porter brings you
an arrogant Greek billionaire whose temporary blindness
leads to an intense relationship with his nurse.

And for all of you who want to be whisked away by
a rich man... *The Secret Baby Bargain*
by Melanie Milburne tells the story of a ruthless
multimillionaire returning to take his ex-fiancée
as his wife. In *The Millionaire's Runaway Bride*
by Catherine George, the electric attraction between
a vulnerable PA and her wealthy ex proves
too tempting to resist.

Finally, we have a brand-new author for you!
In Abby Green's *Chosen as the Frenchman's Bride* a tall,
bronzed Frenchman takes an innocent virgin as his wife.
Be sure to look out for more from Abby very soon!

Dinner at 8

Don't be late!

He's suave and sophisticated.

He's undeniably charming.

And, above all, he treats her like a lady….

But beneath the tux, there's a primal passionate
lover, who's determined to make her his!

Wined, dined and swept away by a
British billionaire!

Catherine George

THE MILLIONAIRE'S RUNAWAY BRIDE

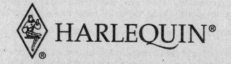

HARLEQUIN®

TORONTO • NEW YORK • LONDON
AMSTERDAM • PARIS • SYDNEY • HAMBURG
STOCKHOLM • ATHENS • TOKYO • MILAN • MADRID
PRAGUE • WARSAW • BUDAPEST • AUCKLAND

ISBN-13: 978-0-373-12625-5
ISBN-10:   0-373-12625-5

THE MILLIONAIRE'S RUNAWAY BRIDE

First North American Publication 2007.

Copyright © 2006 by Catherine George.

www.eHarlequin.com

Printed in U.S.A.

All about the author...
Catherine George

CATHERINE GEORGE was born on the border
between Wales and England in a village blessed
with a library. Catherine was fervently encouraged
to read by a like-minded mother, and early on she
developed an addiction to reading.

At eighteen Catherine met the husband who
eventually took her off to Brazil. He worked as chief
engineer of a large gold-mining operation in Minas
Gerais, which provided a popular background for
several of Catherine's early novels.

After nine happy years, the education of their small
son took them back to Britain, and soon afterward
a daughter was born. But Catherine always
found time to read, if only in the bath! When her
husband's job took him abroad again she enrolled
in a creative-writing course, and then read countless
novels by Harlequin authors before trying a hand at
one herself. Her first effort was not only accepted,
but voted best of its genre for that year.

Catherine has written well over sixty novels since
and has won another award along the way. But now
she has come full circle. After Brazil, and in England
the Wirral, Warwick and the Forest of Dean, the
family home is now the beautiful Welsh Marches—
with access to a county library, several bookshops
and a busy market hall with a treasure trove of
secondhand paperbacks!

CHAPTER ONE

SHE locked the car, and set off at a run past such a long line of parked cars she felt horribly guilty. The party was obviously in full swing and the guest of honour was late. As she raced up the drive towards the house the door flew open, but before Anna Maitland could start scolding Kate gave her a hug and a penitent kiss.

'Sorry, folks,' she panted.

'The late Miss Durant!' Ben Maitland grinned and gave her a bear hug.

Anna elbowed her husband aside. 'You said you were about to leave when I rang, Kate. Where have you *been*?'

'I went on painting too long. And at the last minute I remembered that my party gear was still packed, so I had to wear something that didn't need ironing.' Kate pointed an accusing finger at her friend's clinging beaded dress. 'Hey— just look at that cleavage! You said dress code was casual.'

'*Smart* casual,' scolded Anna, frowning at Kate's jeans.

'Are we going to stand out here all night?' inquired Ben.

'No, indeed—get a move on, Kate,' ordered Anna. 'Take your things up to the spare room.'

Kate saluted smartly, and ran upstairs to dump her bag and toss her coat on the bed. She replaced suede boots with black silk slippers with high silver heels, tugged her silver satin camisole into place and teased a loose strand from her upswept knot of hair. She renewed her lipstick, hung silver and crystal icicles from her ears and ran downstairs to join her friends.

'Smart casual after all, Cinderella,' said Anna, relieved.

'Ready for the fray?' asked Ben.

7

Kate grinned. 'You bet. Lead me to the champagne.'

Anna seized Kate by the hand to tow her through the crowd of people in party mood, taking her on a round of greetings to old acquaintances and introductions to new ones before she left her with a fair, attractive man ordered to take good care of her. Richard Forster was obviously only too happy to do so, and Kate was quickly absorbed into a convivial group, blissfully unaware that she was under surveillance.

In the adjoining conservatory, half concealed by greenery, a man stood answering questions about his company's latest regeneration project. His answers were courteous and informative but his covert attention was on the new arrival. Unlike the other women she wore jeans with some shiny thing that looked like underwear. Her lean, boyish figure had fuller curves above the waist now, but her hair still shone like the conkers they'd once collected under his father's chestnut tree. And, instead of looking the odd one out, she made the other women seem overdressed.

'That's Anna Maitland's friend, Kate Durant,' said the man next to him, following his look. 'Want an introduction?'

Still unaware that she was under scrutiny, Kate sipped champagne and contributed her fair share to the conversation in the group. But when she turned her head slightly her fingers clenched, white-knuckled on her glass, as she recognised the tall man wending his way towards her. The mane of black waving hair was shorter, the build more formidable and the angular planes of the face harder, but one look at him was like a blow to the heart.

'Hello, Katherine,' he said casually, as though it had been days instead of years since their last encounter.

'You've met Jack Logan?' asked Richard Forster, and Kate pulled herself together, smiling with hard-won composure as she held out her hand.

'Why, yes, many moons ago. Hello, Jack. Fancy meeting you here.'

'Kate and I are old friends from way back.' He included the group in his smile as he put a hand under her elbow. 'Forgive me if I steal her away for a minute.'

'Sorry I couldn't introduce you.' She took her arm back once they were out of earshot. 'I didn't get all the names.'

'I know most of them.'

'And they all know you, of course.'

'Big fish, small pool.' His eyes held hers. 'You look good, Kate. A touch rounder these days, but it suits you.'

'Thank you.' Kate peered past him round the room. 'Where's your wife?' she asked pointedly.

His eyes narrowed in surprise. 'She's in Australia.'

'On holiday?'

'Dawn went to live with her sister in Sydney straight after the divorce. She married an Aussie years ago.'

Divorce? Kate covered her stupefaction with a smile. 'I hadn't heard.'

He smiled coldly. 'Can't be easy, keeping track of all your ex-fiancés.'

Her answering smile was colder. 'I can't boast *that* many.'

'And none at the moment, I hear.' His eyes moved over her bare shoulders with a look Kate felt like a brand on her skin.

'Who's your informant?' she asked.

'The Maitlands' next door neighbour, Lucy Beresford. Her husband's company does a lot of electrical work for me. They moved here after you left for the big city.' Jack smiled blandly. 'I didn't tell her I'm on the list of ex-lovers.'

'Why would you?' She gave him a bright, social smile. 'Will you excuse me? Good to talk to you again, Jack, but I must see if Anna needs help.'

Kate stalked into the kitchen, her eyes stormy as she beckoned Anna away from the caterers. 'A word in private, please.'

Anna took one look and chivvied Kate into the pantry and closed the door. 'What's up?'

Kate glared at her friend. 'What on earth possessed you to invite Jack Logan here?'

Anna looked taken aback. 'Why ever shouldn't I? Not that I did invite him,' she added, pulling a face. 'Apparently he gave George Beresford a lift home tonight and Lucy convinced our local celeb I'd be delighted if they brought him along to meet you. My jaw dropped when I found Jack Logan on my doorstep, believe me. He never goes to parties.'

'He only came to this one out of curiosity.' Kate took in a deep breath. 'He's the man I was engaged to before I met you.'

'*What?* You're kidding!' Anna goggled in amazement.

'I haven't seen him since we broke up.' Kate's mouth twisted. 'It was rather a shock to find him here tonight.'

'I bet it was!' Anna shook her head in wonder. 'I was in shock myself. And, gush as I might, my faultless hostess act didn't deceive the man for a second. He knew I felt awful for not inviting him. Anyway, he apologised very charmingly for gatecrashing, and Ben gave him a drink and took him on a round of introductions. But he wouldn't have needed many. Logan Development's a household name round here.' Anna gave her a wicked look. 'You should have stuck with him. He's loaded.'

Kate's eyes flashed ominously. 'We didn't break up over money!'

'I'm sure you didn't.' Anna patted her hand. 'But whatever the reason, don't let it spoil the party for you. This whole shebang is in your honour, remember.'

'I know, and I appreciate it.' Kate gave her an apologetic hug. 'Let me give you a hand with your guests.'

Kate helped her friend supervise while the catering staff served the buffet supper, exchanged banter with those who knew her and pleasantries with others—and without making it obvious managed to avoid Jack Logan entirely. By the time the last guest was served she was beginning to regret her killer heels and agreed with gratitude when Anna filled a plate for her and insisted she take a break.

'Sneak off to the study with this—if those jeans let you eat!'

Kate made her escape along the hall to the study, but almost turned tail again when Jack Logan rose from the sofa, plate in hand.

'Looking for sanctuary?' he asked. 'Maitland rescued me from people determined to talk shop. But I can find somewhere else.'

She shrugged indifferently, and settled behind the desk with her supper. 'Stay if you want.'

He looked amused as she attacked her meal. 'You're obviously hungry.'

'I was too busy to eat lunch today.'

There was a pause while they ate in fraught silence, Kate determined to get the food down, even if it choked her.

'Are you up for the weekend?' Jack asked at last, as though he were a polite stranger instead of the man who'd once broken her heart.

'Longer than that.' Kate munched on a mouthful of cheese torte for a moment. 'Actually,' she said, looking him in the eye, 'I've left London for good. I live here now.'

He stared at her incredulously. 'Alone?'

'No.' She held the hard gaze steadily. 'I live with my niece.'

'Ah, I see.' His eyes softened. 'I was very sorry about your sister. Tragic accident.' He raised a quizzical eyebrow. 'But I'm curious, Kate. What brought you back to this neck of the woods? At one time you couldn't get away fast enough.'

'My aunt left me a house here in Park Crescent. When Elizabeth and Robert were killed—'

'I was at the funeral.'

She stared at him, startled. 'Were you? I didn't see you.'

He shrugged. 'It seemed like a bad time to intrude. But I was there.'

'Why, thank you, Jack, that was very kind,' she said quietly. 'After it was over I brought my niece to stay here with Anna and Ben. Joanna was desperate to leave London after her parents died, and she liked it here so much I resigned my job, sold my flat and moved to Park Crescent to make a home for her.'

'Amazing.' Jack's eyes were cold. 'Not,' he added, 'the admirable aim to make a home for your niece, but to provide it here instead of London. At one time a career there was all you wanted in life. You thought I was mad to stay here and work with my father.'

Kate shrugged. 'It was your choice to make. Mine was different.'

'Obviously the right one. I heard you climbed pretty far up the tree in your job. Was your niece your only reason for leaving it?'

'It was the deciding factor, yes, but I'd had a move in mind for a while. The chain of department stores I worked for merged with a bigger outfit a while back. I stayed on for a year or so after the takeover, but it wasn't the same with the new regime. So when Liz and Robert died I decided to accept the company's very generous pay-off and make a life for Jo back here.'

'So what will you do now? Look for a job here in town?'

'I've already sorted one,' she said, and got up with her empty plate. 'Can I get you some pudding?'

He stood up. 'Let me bring some for you.'

She shook her head. 'No, thanks, Jack, I must get back to the fray. In case you didn't know, Anna gave the party just for me—a sort of welcome home for the prodigal.'

'I did know. Lucy Beresford told me.'

She gave him a mocking smile. 'Yet you still came?'

'It was the sole reason *why* I came. I rarely go to parties, let alone turn up at one uninvited. Tonight curiosity won over manners.' His eyes locked with hers. 'I'm glad it did. It's good to see you again, Kate.'

'You too, Jack.' Kate gave him a cool little smile, and hurried back to the sanctuary of the dining room.

'There you are, Kate.' Anna trickled damson sauce over two plates of hazelnut meringues and handed them over. 'I promised Richard you'd join him to eat these.'

'Richard,' repeated Kate blankly.

'Richard Forster, the man I invited for you!'

'Are you matchmaking again?' said Kate, exasperated. 'Give it up, Anna. It's no sin to be single and thirty-something.'

'Thirty-four, if we're counting,' Anna reminded her. 'And I'm not asking you to marry the man, just talk to him for a bit. You've hardly spoken two words to him yet.'

'Sorry, sorry, situation remedied right now.' Kate went off to hunt down her quarry and found him in the conservatory, looking out at the moonlit garden. 'Hi,' she said, handing him a plate. 'I hope you like this kind of thing.'

In actual fact Richard Forster actively disliked sweet things, but wasn't fool enough to refuse food, or anything else, offered by a woman like Kate Durant.

'Thank you.' He began on his meringues with apparent relish while he asked her how she was settling back into small town life after her years in the capital.

'It's quite an adjustment,' she admitted. 'But I grew up here, so I don't feel totally alien. And I've been so busy with my new job and setting my house to rights I haven't had time to miss my old life. Friends and colleagues, yes, but not the hours I put in, or the endless meetings.'

'I'm with you there,' he said with feeling. 'Until recently I worked in a City law practice.'

'What brought you back here?'

His face shadowed. 'My father's health began to deteriorate. I left London to lighten his load in the family firm.'

'Of course.' Kate clicked her fingers. 'That's why the name rang a bell—your father was my aunt's solicitor. He's been very helpful to me.'

'Great man, my dad.' He smiled at her. 'So, Miss Durant, you and I have something in common; we're both newly returned to the fold.'

'Has settling back here been hard for you?'

He sobered abruptly. 'Afraid so. My wife didn't settle back with me.'

'Oh.' Kate smiled in quick sympathy. 'I'm sorry.'

He nodded. 'Me too. I felt very strongly about joining my father but Caroline felt equally so about keeping her job in London. So now we're a statistic; one more marriage heading for the rocks.' He smiled ruefully. 'Sorry! That was more than you wanted to know.'

He was right there, thought Kate with a pang of guilt. Years ago she had refused to stay here with Jack for a not too different reason. She thrust the memory away and smiled warmly at Richard.

'Can I tempt you to more pudding?'

'No, thanks,' he said hastily, and took her empty plate. 'My turn. I'll fetch coffee.'

Kate moved behind a concealing fern, glad of a moment alone to get herself together. Just seeing Jack Logan again had been shock enough, but the news that he'd been divorced for years was shattering. No surprise in some ways; straight, attractive men of Jack's age—and Richard Forster's—were rarely just plain single. But Richard was clearly still affected by his break-up, while she doubted very much that Jack's recovery had taken long. Her eyes kindled. Lord knew it had taken him no time at all to find someone else after she'd left for London. Whereas she'd taken years to get over Jack Logan. She gazed out over the moonlit garden with nostalgia.

She'd been so young and so madly in love… She tensed, the hairs standing up on her neck when a voice spoke in her ear.

'Why are you hiding in here?'

She felt Jack's breath, warm on her skin, and turned sharply. 'Waiting for my coffee to arrive.' She looked past him, smiling brightly as Richard joined them.

'I was told you like yours black and sweet, Kate,' he informed her, handing her a cup. 'Can I bring some for you, Logan?'

'Good of you, but no thanks, I'm leaving,' said Jack. 'I just came to say goodnight.'

'Goodbye, then. So nice to see you again,' Kate said politely.

Jack nodded to them both and strolled off to find his hostess. Kate stared after his tall, commanding figure for a moment then turned to Richard with a smile. 'Jack and I were friends a long time ago.'

'So I gather,' he said wryly, well aware that there'd been a lot more than just friendship between them. And Jack Logan still wanted it.

Jack could have confirmed this. After leaving the party he'd felt a crazy impulse to head for Park Crescent to wait for Kate. But common sense warned that a brandy before bed was a better idea than hanging about outside her house in the small hours only to find that someone else had brought her home— Forster, probably. Or she could be staying the night with the Maitlands. His mouth twisted in sudden derision. It was unlikely she'd have fallen into his arms if he had lain in wait for her. But his body's reaction to even the thought of it made it plain that he still wanted her. He always had, from the moment he'd first set eyes on her.

Kate had been standing on the steps of the Guildhall, selling poppies for Remembrance Day. She'd accosted him with a smile, rattling her tin when he parked near her pitch. He'd bought the biggest poppy on her tray and on impulse presented it to her with a bow, and she'd blushed. Jack had never seen a girl blush so vividly before. He'd stared, fascinated by the tide of colour, but more people came up to buy poppies, he was late for an appointment, and when he returned to his car later she'd gone.

Back in the cold, dark present Jack Logan pressed a remote control and drove through tall iron gates along a winding drive to the stables he'd converted to a garage when he'd first started developing the property. At that turning point in his life, with a broken engagement, a hasty marriage and even hastier divorce under his belt, he'd made a conscious decision to steer clear of close relationships with women in future. From that day forward all his passions would be channelled into expanding the family building firm.

When he first bought the Mill House property his original plan had been to get rid of the house itself and use the land for one of the mixed housing projects that were rapidly winning Logan Development a respected name. But the almost derelict house, sleeping at the centre of wild overgrown grounds, cast such a spell on him he couldn't bring himself to demolish it. Instead he put the property on the back burner and concentrated on more pressing projects. When he eventually turned his attention to Mill House he'd planned to make it into a show house as an advertisement for the company's restoration skills before putting it up for sale. But the process of converting a virtual ruin into a dreamhouse backfired on him. While the house was slowly, carefully restored, and the land around it tamed and nurtured, he'd looked from tall windows at a seductive view of mill pond and chestnut trees and felt a sense of possession almost as fierce as the emotion once experienced for Kate. When the work was completed Mill House was so much his own creation it was impossible to let someone else live there.

Jack unlocked the boot room at the back of the house and

bent to pat the black retriever who came rushing in exuberant welcome to meet him. He let Bran out into the garden for a quick run and stood at the door, eyes absent on the moon's reflection in the water. After a few minutes he whistled and the dog shot back inside, getting underfoot in the kitchen as Jack made coffee in preference to fetching the brandy decanter. He sat down at the table to drink it and scratched Bran's ears, his smile wry as he looked down into the adoring eyes. Canine love was a lot easier to deal with than the human variety.

In bed later Jack gave up any pretence of trying to sleep. Normally he never allowed himself to dwell on the past, but one look at Kate tonight had opened a mental door that refused to slam shut.

Logan and Son had already won recognition as the town's premier building contractor when Jack's father sent him to make an estimate for a house extension. While Jack was making notes of the owner's requirements the kitchen door burst open and Kate had come running in, slender and coltish in T-shirt and jeans, bright hair flying.

She'd stopped dead at the sight of the visitor, colour high. 'Oh—sorry. Didn't know we had visitors.'

'It's all right, dear,' said Robert Sutton, and introduced the girl as his sister-in-law, Katherine Durant.

Jack held out his hand. 'I'm the son in Logan and Son,' he said, smiling, and Kate put her hand in his.

'I'm Kate,' she said breathlessly. 'I sold you a poppy the other day.'

'I remember.' Conscious that Robert Sutton was watching them like a hawk, Jack returned to facts and figures and Kate left them to it. To his intense disappointment she was nowhere to be seen when he left the house, but as he drove out into the road his heart leapt at the sight of Kate walking a little way ahead. He halted alongside and rolled the car window down. 'Can I give you a lift?'

She smiled demurely. 'How kind of you.'

On the way into town Jack learned that Kate had just celebrated her twentieth birthday. After a business course at the local college, she was currently temping with local firms while making applications for something permanent in London.

'Now you,' she ordered.

Jack told her he was four years her senior, with a degree in civil engineering, and had worked for a big name construction company during university vacations to gain experience. 'But my aim was always to join my father's firm once I had the education part out of the way,' he told her. 'Dad and I make a good team. Business is booming. Where shall I drop you?' he added, and from the corner of his eye saw familiar colour rise in her face.

'Confession time,' she admitted reluctantly. 'I wasn't going anywhere. I lurked in the road to—well, to ambush you. Just drop me anywhere convenient and I'll walk back.'

Bewitched by her honesty, Jack turned into the car park of the Rose and Crown. 'Have lunch with me first.'

She smiled at him radiantly. 'I'd love to!'

Their first meal together was a sandwich and a glass of lager, but to both of them it was nectar and ambrosia as they sat in a corner of the crowded bar, so absorbed in each other they could have been on a desert island. It was over an hour before Jack remembered to look at his watch.

'Hell, I must get back to work. But I'll drive you home first.'

'Absolutely not. I'll walk back.' Kate looked up at him anxiously as they reached the car. 'You probably think I had the most awful nerve, lying in wait for you like that.'

He'd smiled down into the dark eyes fastened on his as though his answer was a matter of life and death. 'I couldn't believe my luck,' he assured her huskily, and clenched his hands to stop them reaching for her. 'Are you free this evening?'

Later that night, after a session in the cinema more like hours of foreplay to Jack, he parked in a lane on the way back to Kate's home, ready to explode if he didn't kiss her, and almost before he could switch off the engine she was in his arms and his mouth was on hers. They devoured each other greedily, kissing and caressing until neither could breathe and the inside of the car was like a sauna.

'You're killing me,' groaned Jack. 'But I'll die a happy man—almost.'

Kate rubbed her cheek against his, threading her fingers through his thick black hair. 'What would it take to make you really happy?'

'Honestly?'

'Honestly!'

He cupped her face in fierce hands. 'To get you naked, kiss every inch of you and make love until we're both brainless.'

Shivering in delight at the thought, Kate licked the tip of her tongue round her parted lips and Jack growled and began kissing her again. At last he thrust her away with unsteady hands and fastened her seat belt.

'Does your sister know you're out with me?' he demanded.

'Of course,' she said breathlessly, and slanted a sparkling look at him. 'Elizabeth is looking forward to meeting you.'

Jack swallowed. 'Really?'

'Don't panic.' She gave a wicked chuckle. 'She only wants you to finish her extension quickly!'

From the first they saw as much of each other as Jack's workload allowed, and he made a point of visiting the Sutton house regularly once work was underway to make sure the extension was completed in good time. His aim was to impress Kate's family with his firm's work, and at the same time convince them that Jack Logan was a suitable husband for her. To his relief Elizabeth and Robert approved of both, and gave their blessing when he eventually asked permission to marry Kate.

Looking on her consent as a mere formality, Jack had proposed, supremely confident that Kate was so much in love with him she would forget her ambitions about a job in London.

What a fool! He flung out of bed to stand at his window, staring savagely at the night sky. Kate had been thrilled to wear his mother's engagement ring, and deliriously happy to make plans for a wedding.

'In the meantime,' she told him eagerly, 'you can apply for jobs in London. You could start with the construction company you worked for before—'

'Hey! Hold on, Kate,' he interrupted, frowning. 'I have no intention of working in London.'

'But Jack,' she said, taken aback, 'you'll have to when I get a job there.'

'Look, sweetheart,' he said, trying hard to be reasonable, 'Dad and I have big plans for Logan and Son. Even if I wanted to, which I most definitely do not, I couldn't desert him now, just when things are really starting to take off.'

Kate stared at him in blank dismay. 'But you've always known what I wanted to do.'

Jack held on to his temper with difficulty. 'I *thought* you wanted to marry me.'

'I do want to marry you! But I want a career in London at the same time. We could both have one, Jack.' She looked at him in pleading. 'I'm sure your father wouldn't hold you back if he knew how you feel.'

'You mean how *you* feel,' Jack told her shortly, then took her by the shoulders before laying it on the line. 'Listen, Kate, I couldn't stand being a little cog in some big company's machine. I want to build up my own outfit, not just for my father's sake, but for mine. I intend to run my own show one day. If you love me, stay and help me.'

But Kate was already sliding the ring from her finger, tears pouring down her face as she held it out. 'I do love you— I'm crazy about you. But you'd better hang on to the ring for a while because I really need to *do* something with my life before I settle down here for good. I'm not ready for that yet, Jack.'

Too proud and hurt to argue, Jack had put the ring away and driven Kate home, sure that parting without even a good-night kiss would make her so miserable she'd change her mind by morning. But the morning post had brought Kate requests for interviews from two London-based companies. Soon afterwards she was accepted by one of them as a management trainee, and rang Jack in excitement to tell him. He wished her good luck, but to her utter dismay refused to meet her to celebrate.

'I don't see the point,' he said tersely. 'You've made your choice, and I'm keeping to mine.'

'Shall I see you when I'm down next, then?'

But proud, obstinate and desperately hurt, Jack answered in a way that changed both their lives. 'No point in that either, in the circumstances.'

He heard her draw in a deep, unsteady breath, and waited, his tension mounting. 'I see,' she said in a dead little voice. 'If that's how you feel we'd better make it a clean break, then. Goodbye.'

Three months later Jack married Dawn Taylor, daughter of the landlord of the Rose and Crown.

CHAPTER TWO

In Anna's guest room Kate lay equally sleepless, wishing she'd gone home. At least there she could have made tea, or gone on painting her sitting room. She sighed and thumped her pillow for the umpteenth time. It was Jack Logan's fault. Though to be fair, she reminded herself irritably, chance encounters with him were factors she'd dismissed as unimportant when she made the decision to return here. During her one visit home after leaving to start the new job she hadn't tried to contact him, and Robert and Elizabeth had moved to London soon afterwards. Kate's next visit had been years later, when the Maitlands bought a house in the area after Ben was head-hunted by a firm of local architects. There'd been occasional visits to Anna and Ben since, but from the day she'd given his ring back Kate had never laid eyes on Jack Logan again until tonight.

She stared into the darkness. He'd changed quite a bit. Which was no surprise. He'd packed a lot into his life in the years since their last meeting—not only the hard work which had brought him such meteoric success, but marriage and divorce along the way. Kate's eyes kindled. She was human enough to feel glad his marriage hadn't lasted. She'd never been able to think of it without a stab of pain. Jack had broken her heart in pieces when he married Dawn Taylor.

Kate was still thinking about this when she went downstairs next morning to make tea. The house was quiet and the kitchen immaculate, all traces of the party removed the night before by the catering firm. She looked up with a smile as Anna came in, yawning.

'I thought I heard you, Kate. Why so early?'

'I didn't get much sleep last night. Nothing to do with the bed,' Kate added hastily.

'But a lot to do with Jack Logan. Sorry, love, if I'd had the least idea that *he* was the secret lover—'

'Ex-lover.'

'Whatever. I'd have given you advance warning.'

'Did you know about his divorce?'

'No; I don't know much about him at all, other than his success with these restoration projects of his. Everything he touches seems to turn to gold. They call it Logan's luck hereabouts according to Ben.' Anna shook her head in wonder. 'To think it was Jack Logan's name that never sullied your lips!'

'What have you been reading lately?' said Kate, smiling, then pulled a face. 'Lord, I felt like such a fool when I asked about his wife. I wonder why the lovely Dawn left him.'

'No idea. Ask Jack.'

'As if!'

'Are you going to see him again?'

'I doubt it.' Kate sniffed. 'He was a touch pejorative about my track record in the romance department.'

'But engagements were your speciality. At least you never got married—and divorced—like him.' Anna looked speculative. 'There's no one significant in his life right now, though. According to Lucy Beresford—the fount of all knowledge—the eligible Jack Logan lives all by himself in that showplace of his.'

'Amazing. When I saw that article about it in the Sunday magazine I took it for granted Dawn lived there with him.'

'They must have split up before he developed the property.' Anna downed her tea at the sound of footsteps upstairs 'Stand by your beds! Ben's on the move at last.'

'I'll just wait to say hello and goodbye, then I'm off home,' said Kate, and smiled. 'Home. That sounds so good, Anna.'

'You owned the flat in Notting Hill.'

'True, but I never thought of it as anything but a temporary arrangement, somehow. But, thanks to darling Aunt Edith, I now have a home worthy of the name. And, most important of all, Jo loves it as much as I do.'

When Kate reached Park Crescent she stayed in the car for a moment, gazing in satisfaction at her inheritance. The house was a small gem of early Victorian architecture with white walls, bay windows and a dark blue door with a fanlight and stone pediment. Mine, all mine, gloated Kate as she locked her car and went inside. She scooped up the Sunday paper on the way to the room her aunt had always referred to as the parlour, and smiled, pleased, as she examined her handiwork. The wall she'd painted the day before was the exact shade she'd been aiming for now it was dry—somewhere between cream and muted pink—or Coral Porcelain as it said on the tin. A perfect background for the white-painted 1857 fire grate.

Interior decorating was new in Kate's life. Jo had helped choose furniture and pore over paint cards, Ben had given invaluable advice; Anna had been forthcoming, as usual, with her own opinions and Kate had been grateful to all of them. But the end result, she thought with satisfaction, was mostly her own.

She read a few pages of the Sunday paper over breakfast in the kitchen she'd had refitted before she moved in, then, rather lacking in enthusiasm after her sleepless night, went upstairs to change into jeans and sweatshirt ready for her daily session with a paintbrush. She checked her emails and then paused, as she always did, to look at the view of the lake. She jerked the curtain aside as she spotted a man running through the rain with long, ground-eating strides, a black dog loping beside him as they skirted the lake. Jack! Kate watched as he slowed down to a walk, the dog, a retriever, she noted enviously, padding obediently beside him. She dodged back in anticipation, sure Jack was making for Park Crescent. And

felt like a complete fool when he unlocked a mud-splashed
Cherokee Jeep near the park gate, loaded the wet dog inside
and drove off. She was too busy for visitors anyway, she told
herself irritably, and ran downstairs to open a tin of paint.

When Elizabeth and Robert Sutton moved to London Kate
had lived with them at first. But after Joanna was born she
eventually left the Sutton household to share a flat with Anna
Travers. The two girls were kindred spirits from the moment
Kate answered Anna's advertisement for a flatmate, and lived
together in complete accord right up to the day Anna married
Ben and then moved away, at which point Kate gave in to
her current boyfriend's urging. Her feelings for David
Houston were nothing like the passion she'd felt for Jack
Logan, but Jack was long since married and she was long
since over him, so she accepted David's proposal and moved
in with him. But eventually their relationship wound down to
an amicable end, and Kate exchanged the brick walls and
leather and chrome of David's hip Thames-side loft for a
small flat of her own at last in Notting Hill.

At that stage Kate's life was as close to ideal as she could
make it. She moved swiftly up the ladder in her job, enjoyed
a lively social life, spent her Sundays in her sister's household
and remained on friendly terms with David. This well-ordered
phase of her life went on until she met Rupert Chance, heir
to a chain of supermarkets. He singled her out at a party and
instantly began a relentless pursuit she was human enough to
find flattering. He soon began persuading her to share his
house in Chelsea, but Kate held back. She was attracted to
the persuasive Rupert but caution prompted her to wait before
burning her boats. Byronic good looks coupled with effortless
charm had always won Rupert Chance anything he wanted
the moment he wanted it, and he objected strongly when Kate
insisted on keeping to her own flat. When they were married,
he informed her, things would change.

Drastic changes came before that, in a way neither of them

could have foreseen. Edith Durant, elder sister of Kate's father, died at the age of ninety-one, and in her will left money to her niece Elizabeth and her house and contents to her younger niece, Katherine. Elizabeth and Robert Sutton celebrated their windfall with a luxury holiday during Joanna's autumn term, but died together when their hired car swerved off a mountain road during a storm.

Kate broke the news to Jo. She drove down to the school, held the child in her arms while she cried her heart out, and in her capacity as official guardian arranged for Joanna to take time off after the funeral. When the service was over Kate took Jo to stay overnight with Robert's elderly, grief-stricken parents, then on to Anna and Ben to recuperate. Their support was a great comfort while the child struggled to come to terms with her loss, and during their week's stay Kate took Joanna to see the house in Park Crescent. The child fell in love with it and, after much discussion, the decision was made to move from London. Instead of selling Aunt Edith's house they would live in it together, in the town where Joanna's mother and aunt had grown up.

The Notting Hill flat had been expensive to buy but with the improvements Kate had made over the years proved profitable to sell. The proceeds were enough to renovate and furnish the house in Park Crescent, and leave enough over for a respectable nest egg to cushion Kate's altered lifestyle. Joanna's education had been provided for since her birth, and her inheritance from her parents, along with the proceeds from the sale of their house, was carefully invested to provide for the future. Kate was determined to make life as happy and secure for the child as humanly possible.

Kate finished a tin of paint with a feeling of satisfaction for a job well done and called it a day. She soaked in scented hot water later with a heartfelt sigh of pleasure. Another wall had been painted and she'd taken it in her stride when Jack Logan drove off instead of calling in to see her. Her shrug rippled the water. No point in getting uptight. Casual sightings could be a fact of life from now on. She could run into Jack anywhere and any time. It was not a problem.

Anna rang later while Kate was getting dressed. 'Hi. How's it going?'

Kate reported on her painting progress, but Anna brushed that aside.

'How are you, really?'

'A bit tired, but I've had a long, lazy bath—'

'I meant after meeting the old flame!'

'Fine. Why shouldn't I be?'

'Not even a little bit singed round the edges?'

'Not in the slightest.'

'Thank goodness,' said Anna, relieved. 'Sleep well.'

Kate dried her hair, left it loose on her shoulders and took some coffee upstairs to the study at present doubling as both workplace and sitting room until her decorating was finished. She drew the curtains, switched on lamps and, with a sigh of satisfaction, curled up in the armchair to read the rest of the Sunday papers before supper. She frowned in surprise when the doorbell rang shortly afterwards. She got up to peer down from the window and saw a long, sleek car parked at the kerb and an all too familiar male figure standing under her exterior light. She went downstairs, fixed a polite smile on her face and opened the door to Jack Logan.

Her visitor loomed tall on her doorstep, looking very different from the night before in a battered leather windbreaker and jeans. He smiled, raking a hand through hair ruffled by the wind blowing along the street from the lake. 'Hello, Kate. I took a chance on finding you at home. May I come in?'

'Of course.' She led him along the hall to the kitchen and pulled out one of the kitchen chairs. 'Nowhere else to receive visitors yet, I'm afraid. Would you like coffee, or a drink?'

'Coffee would be good. Thank you.' Jack leaned against the counter, his eyes on the fall of burnished hair as he watched Kate get to work. 'I went for a run in the park with the dog this morning, intending to call on you afterwards, but Bran and I were so wet I decided against it.'

This information won him a warmer smile. 'Have you had the dog long?'

'Five years.' Jack slung his jacket on the back of a chair. 'He's a black retriever—great company. When I'm not around, Dad takes care of him.'

'How *is* your father?' Kate made the coffee, set the pot and a pair of mugs on the table and fetched sugar and milk, glad of homely occupation while she adjusted to Jack Logan's dominant presence in her kitchen.

'Dad's semi-retired, plays a lot of golf these days.' He smiled. 'I hoped he'd marry again, but I'm afraid he's a one-woman man.'

Which was more than could be said for his son, thought Kate with rancour. 'I was very fond of your father.'

'The feeling was mutual.'

She shot him a look. 'That can't have lasted once we split up.'

'You mean when you took off for London rather than marry me!' Their eyes clashed for a moment, then Jack shrugged. 'Actually my father was a lot more tolerant than me. He told me to give you time to spread your wings. But for me it was all or nothing.'

'You can't say you pined for long!'

'Actually, you're wrong about that.' Jack crossed his legs and sat back, surveying her thoughtfully. 'Maybe it's time you knew the truth.'

Kate shook her head as she poured coffee. 'No need, Jack. I chose to leave, and you married Dawn on the rebound. These things happen.'

'Not in the way you think.'

She gave him an assessing look, resentful that the lines on his face merely added character to the good looks of his youth. 'I don't think about it, Jack. It was a long time ago. No point in raking it all up again.'

'I look on it as setting the record straight.' He drank some of his coffee, then set down the mug. 'After you took off for London,' he said, with the air of a man determined to have his say, 'I began drowning my sorrows at the Rose and Crown most nights, and Dawn Taylor offered the kind of comfort I was fool enough to accept eventually, because I was so bloody miserable without you. But when she begged me to marry her because she was pregnant, I realised exactly what kind of a fool I'd been. Dawn was very popular with her father's punters, and Dad said I was an idiot to believe that the child was mine.' He gave her a straight look. 'Nevertheless, it could have been mine, Kate.'

She held his eyes. 'What happened to the baby?'

'Dawn miscarried soon after the wedding, eighteen weeks into the pregnancy.' His mouth twisted. 'My entire relationship with Dawn up to that point, including the marriage, added up to twelve weeks. You can do the maths.'

'So who *was* the father?'

'Someone else's husband.' Jack shrugged. 'So in a panic Dawn told me the baby was mine, hoping to pass it off on me as premature. When it all went horribly wrong she agreed to a quickie divorce and used my one-off settlement to visit her sister in Australia. I haven't seen her since.'

Kate digested this in silence for a while. 'She was a very pretty girl—spectacular figure,' she said at last, and looked at him very directly. 'It broke my heart when you married her so soon after we split up.'

His eyes hardened. 'You broke mine when you took off for London.'

'Oh, come on, Jack,' she retorted. 'London wasn't the moon. I could have come home to you every weekend right from the start, or you could have come to me, but not a chance. It had to be your way or nothing.'

'I changed my mind pretty quickly,' he said, startling her. 'I missed you like hell. I soon wanted you back on any terms. I was about to get in touch to tell you that, but Dawn got in first with her news.'

'You mean you expected me to rush back to you even though you slept with her the minute I left?' Kate eyed him coldly. 'I would have found out sooner or later. News travels fast in a small town like this.'

He shrugged. 'Not so very fast, apparently. You didn't know about the divorce.'

'I was living in London then, remember. And if they knew about it, Liz and Robert never told me.'

'Obviously not. But I'm surprised that the news hasn't filtered through to you since.' He smiled wryly. 'Talking of surprises, Anna Maitland looked thunderstruck last night when I gatecrashed her party.'

Kate nodded. 'Because you never go to parties, it didn't occur to her to invite you.'

'Does she know about our relationship?'

'As from last night she does. Anna knew I'd been engaged before I met her, but not the name of the lucky man. I couldn't believe my eyes when you strolled up at the party.' Kate smiled politely. 'But I'm glad you called in tonight, Jack. It gives me a chance to congratulate you on your success.'

'Thank you. We both achieved our aims, career-wise.' He eyed her quizzically. 'But I'm curious, Kate. I'm told you were on the point of marriage twice over the years. What made you back off?'

She hesitated for a moment, then decided it was fair return for Jack's explanation. 'The first fiancé—'

'Second,' he corrected.

She ground her teeth. 'All right, the *second* fiancé started talking about babies and a place in the country.'

'Ah!' Jack leaned back, eyes gleaming. 'The idea didn't appeal?'

'Not in the slightest. So we agreed—amicably—to call it a day, and I bought a flat in Notting Hill. I'd never lived alone up to that point, and enjoyed it so much that years later when I met the second—sorry, *third* fiancé, I insisted on keeping to my own place instead of moving in with him.' Kate looked away. 'A good decision, as it turned out—less complications when we split up.'

'Amicably again?'

'No. More coffee?'

'Thank you.'

Kate got up and filled the kettle again. 'Would you like something to eat? Anna gave me some leftovers.'

Jack shook his head. 'No, thanks, I had dinner with my father earlier. Tell me what happened to fiancé mark three.'

Her eyes shuttered. 'I'd rather not talk about that.'

'Then let's talk about your new job, instead. Will you be working in the town?'

She shook her head, smiling. 'Right here in my study upstairs.'

His eyebrows rose. 'You're writing a novel?'

'I wish! I'm a VA.' She chuckled at his blank look. 'A Virtual Assistant, Jack. Keep up! My computer skills are good, and I was a personal assistant for a while earlier on in my career. But this time I'll be working part-time at home for a handful of clients instead of full-time in an office for just one boss. I choose which people I take on and no coffee-making required for any of them.'

Jack looked sceptical. 'A pretty drastic career change! Are you sure you're cut out for it?'

'Absolutely. I started it up before I left London.' She described her enrolment on a VA Mastery Course the moment she gave in her notice. While she was selling her flat and organising the move, Kate completed the course, set up her personal website, named it KD Virtual Assistance, and asked Anna to advertise it in the local papers back home. Within weeks Kate had three clients, and by the time she'd moved into Park Crescent she had two more.

'I work for people who've set up their own businesses, but lack the time, or inclination, to spare for the administrative side. I meet each of them in person occasionally, of course, so it's not all virtual,' she told Jack. 'I do their invoicing, maintain databases, book appointments, make travel arrangements, or even just deal with household accounts. I won't earn anything like the salary I had before, obviously, but my services don't come cheap. Even working only twenty hours or so a week will give me enough income to live on and, most important of all, I'll be here all the time for Joanna when she gets home for the school holidays. She's boarding at the moment.'

'Twenty hours isn't much to someone of your calibre. What will you do with your spare time?'

'All the things I've never had time to do before—my own interior decorating, for one. Something new for me.' She smiled as she poured more coffee. 'I'm enjoying it. But if time begins to hang really heavy I'll take on more clients.'

The slate-grey eyes gleamed over the rim of the mug. 'So if I contacted your website I could ask you to work for me?'

She looked at him steadily. 'You could ask, but I'd refuse.'

'Why?'

'Oh, come on, Jack! You and I come with two much past history to make even a virtual partnership feasible.'

'You can't forgive my trespasses?'

'Surely we can forgive each other after all this time?' she countered. 'We're different people now.'

He eyed her in slow appraisal. 'You don't look different, Kate. With your hair down you look no older than the last time we met.'

'Flatterer!'

'Not at all.' He downed the last of his coffee and got up. 'Time I was off.'

'Thank you for coming, Jack.'

'My pleasure.' He shrugged on his windbreaker, sniffing the air as they went into the hall. 'Fresh paint?'

'In here.' Kate opened the door to the sitting room. 'Joanna's choice of colour and my handiwork. What do you think?'

Jack nodded in approval. 'It looks good. How about furniture?'

'Aunt Edith left me a houseful, but I auctioned some of it. I bought the rest locally, and asked for a delay in delivery until I finish painting. I sold my London furniture with the flat. It seemed the right time to make a fresh start.'

'Off with the old and on with the new?'

'Exactly.' She smiled coolly. 'We're both old hands at that, Jack.'

He shook his head, his eyes narrowed to an unsettling gleam. 'You're the one who gets through fiancés, Kate. I've only had one.'

'That doesn't count—you had a wife.'

He shook his head. 'Dawn doesn't count, either. I married her out of obligation, not love. Did you love the men in your life?'

'Not enough to marry them, obviously.' She brushed past him to the door and opened it. 'But I'm glad I know the truth at last. Thank you for making the effort to put me straight, Jack.'

'No effort involved, Kate,' he assured her and strolled across the pavement to his car. 'Thanks for the coffee. Goodnight.'

'Goodnight.' She waited politely until the car moved off, then went back to the kitchen to scowl at the assortment of party leftovers in the fridge. She put a selection on her plate, cut some bread and slumped down at the table, irritated because Jack had left without asking to see her again. Yet she'd been utterly convinced, right up to the last minute, that this had been the real purpose of his visit. She had wanted—craved—the glorious satisfaction of turning him down. More fool you, Kate, she thought scornfully, and doggedly munched through her supper without tasting a mouthful of it.

CHAPTER THREE

JACK LOGAN'S revelations gave Kate such a restless night she lingered longer than usual with the morning paper over breakfast next morning. She wrote a letter to Joanna afterwards, then finally got to work on reports for two of her clients and chased up late payments for another. She smiled in satisfaction as she shut down her computer. The great advantage of her new job was working at her own speed instead of to the hectic timetable of her former life. Like Jack, colleagues had asked what on earth she was going to do with herself. Work for half the day and then do as she liked, had been Kate's answer. She would take up tennis again, swim, go to a gym regularly instead of once in a blue moon, visit the local cinema and repertory theatre, enjoy Sunday lunch with the Maitlands, look up old friends, and gradually become part of the local scene again.

Anna rang before Kate started painting after lunch. 'Are you busy?'

'Why?'

'I need to see you. Could you possibly down whatever tools you're using and come over for tea?'

'Of course.'

When Anna let her in later Kate studied her friend closely. 'What's up?'

'I'll tell you in a minute. Thanks for coming, love.'

'Any time.' Kate followed her friend into the kitchen. 'It's the big plus of my new occupation. I can drop everything and run if necessary. Though Jack doesn't think much of my change of career,' she added casually.

'Jack?' said Anna instantly. 'You've seen him since the party?'

'He called in last night.'

'Surprise, surprise!' Anna nodded sagely as she made tea. 'Was the visit for old times' sake—or new ones?'

'Old. He came to tell me exactly why he married someone else in such a rush. Usual reason—Dawn was pregnant.'

'By him?'

'No, as it turned out, but it could have been. Jack was merely top of Dawn's sperm-donor list.'

Anna's eyes widened. 'She conned him!'

Kate explained about the miscarriage too far along into the pregnancy for Jack to be the father.

'So that explains the instant divorce. And,' added Anna thoughtfully, 'the lack of significant others in his life since, maybe.'

'There must have been some along the way. I can't see Jack leading the life of a monk!'

'You mean he's terrific in bed? Those dark, smouldering types usually are. Not,' Anna added hastily, 'that I speak from experience. At least not since I met Ben.' She shook her head in wonder as she filled teacups. 'Amazing! All those times I met Jack Logan at the functions Ben drags me to I never knew he was your mystery lover.'

'You adore going to functions with Ben!'

Anna nodded sheepishly. 'Of course I do. I love standing round with a drink making small talk—the sign of a trivial mind, I suppose.'

Kate laughed. 'The man you worked for didn't agree with that. He married you!'

'True. Ben said he was attracted to my razor-sharp mind before he noticed the packaging. Liar!' Anna giggled, then sobered abruptly, her eyes anxious. 'Are you really all right?'

'I'm fine.' Kate reached out a hand to touch Anna's. 'Jack just came round to set the record straight.'

'Did he ask to see you again?'

'No.' Kate grinned ruefully. 'Which really ticked me off. I was so looking forward to turning him down.'

'You still have feelings for him?'

Kate shrugged. 'If I do, I don't know what they are. But when I moved back here I knew I risked running into Jack some time. Though I didn't expect to in this house,' she added tartly.

'Tell me about it!' Anna made a face. 'Lucy Beresford thought it was such a coup for me, bringing him here, because normally he only graces the official functions I told you about, and corporate stuff. But Ben says he turns up at the occasional golf club dinner.'

'To please his father,' said Kate, nodding.

'I suppose that was his reason all those years ago when he wouldn't try for a job in London.'

'Not a bit of it. Jack was pleasing himself.'

'Do I detect an acid note?'

Kate's mouth turned down. 'I was so sure he loved me enough to come to London with me. Anyway,' she added briskly, 'that's all in the past. Now then, you asked me here for a reason. Spill the beans!'

'OK,' said Anna, with an odd little smile. 'I saw my doctor this morning.'

'Why? What's wrong?'

'Nothing, unless you count morning sickness—I'm officially pregnant!'

'Anna, how marvellous!' Kate gave a crow of triumph and hugged her friend affectionately. 'After all these years! How does Ben feel about it?'

'Thrilled to bits—so am I!'

'Me, too.' Kate patted her friend's cheek. 'I'm very happy for you. And so is Ben, by the display of flowers in the hall.'

'Actually,' said Anna, fluttering her eyelashes, 'those are not from my husband.'

'Don't tell me they're from someone else's!'

'Certainly not.' Anna grinned like the Cheshire cat. 'Mr Jack Logan sent them with his apologies and thanks.'

On the way back into town Kate felt oddly restless and wished she'd given in to Anna's coaxing to stay to dinner. There was no work to catch up on that couldn't be dealt with tomorrow.

For the rest of the week Kate's feeling of anticipation dwindled gradually as each day wore on with no word from Jack. By Thursday her sitting room was finished, along with her hopes of hearing from him again. Get over it, she ordered herself.

The chaise longue arrived next morning with perfect timing, just as Kate finished her daily stint at the computer, and tempted by the sunshine she decided to fit in a quick walk in the park before lunch. When she reached the lake path Kate's heart leapt as she spotted a tall figure with a black dog in the distance, but as she drew nearer saw that the man's hair was grey. As if Jack would be taking a stroll on a Friday morning, she told herself scornfully, then smiled in sudden delight as the man straightened from unfastening the dog's leash.

'Katherine!' said Tom Logan, with such obvious pleasure as he caught sight of her she felt her throat thicken.

'Mr Logan—how lovely to see you,' she said huskily, and ran into the arms thrown wide to embrace her.

'Jack told me you were back in town,' he informed her and held her at arms' length to look at her. 'How are you?'

'I'm very well.' She smiled at him affectionately. 'No need to ask how you are. You look marvellous.'

'Semi-retirement suits me,' he agreed. He whistled, and the dog raced back to sit obediently to have his leash attached. 'Good boy.' Tom Logan patted the gleaming black head. 'Are you in a hurry, Kate, or will you walk a little way with us?'

'I'd love to.' Kate bent to pat the dog. 'What a handsome lad.'

'Apple of Jack's eye.' Tom shot a look at her as they began walking. 'And good company for him. Other than Bran and me, Jack's cleaner is the only one to set foot in that house of his.'

'I thought someone in his position would need to entertain a lot.'

'He keeps to restaurants for that. But he's been in London all this week.' The keen eyes, so like his son's, surveyed Kate with interest.

'Has he?' she said casually.

'Didn't he say? Jack told me he called to see you the other night.'

'The conversation centred on past history.' She kept her eyes on the path. 'He told me about Dawn Taylor.'

'God, what a disaster that was,' said Tom grimly. 'But try not to blame Jack too much. After you left he was desperately unhappy, Kate. He missed you so much he worked himself into the ground all day and every day, with a couple of drinks in the Rose and Crown on the way home to help him sleep. Dawn was lying in wait for him every time of course, only too willing to console him, so the result was inevitable. I told him he was a fool to accept the child as his but, as you know better than anyone, Kate, my son can be as obstinate as a mule. So he married her.'

She gave him a questioning look. 'Do you blame me for that, Mr Logan?'

He stared at her, surprised. 'Good God, no, child. You were young, and it was only natural you wanted to see a bit of the world before you settled down. The two of you could have gone on meeting easily enough now and again.'

'It's all water under the bridge now.' Kate glanced at her watch. 'I must dash—pressing appointment in town after lunch with some curtains.' She smiled at him. 'After your next walk come to my place for coffee. Bring Bran with you. I live in Park Crescent, number thirty-four.'

'So Jack told me.' Tom Logan smiled reminiscently. 'Oddly enough, I know the house well. I did a lot of work for Miss Durant when I first started out on my own. She was one of the old school, a real tartar. But she knew her stuff when it came to maintaining her property. She approved of my work, so we got on well. You inherited a sound house, Kate.' He smiled and patted her cheek affectionately. 'It's so good to see you again, my dear.'

'Likewise, Mr L.'

'I think it's time you called me Tom!'

'Then I will. See you soon, Tom.' She hurried off to the park gate and turned to wave as she passed through to make for home.

Jack Logan felt so tired during the drive from London through heavy Friday evening traffic he rang his father from his hands free moible as he turned off the motorway and asked him to keep Bran for another night. But, after hearing about the encounter with Kate, Jack drove straight past the entrance to Mill House and headed into town, cursing himself for a fool as he parked near Kate's house. The lights were on. But that could mean time switches. The car he'd seen before was parked right outside her house again too, but even if it were hers it meant nothing. She could have taken a taxi into town, or someone—some man—could have picked her up to take her out.

He got out of the car, flexing his shoulders wearily. He rapped on the doorknocker instead of ringing the bell and waited, shivering, until light shone through the fanlight. After a moment Kate opened the door, her face guarded.

'Hello,' he said quietly. 'May I come in?'

Without a word she led the way into the sitting room and switched off the television, eyeing her visitor without visible warmth. 'You look tired, Jack.'

'The traffic was heavy. I rang my father during the journey

and heard he'd seen you today.' He gave her a wry, weary smile. 'So I took a chance on finding you in.'

Kate's feelings were mixed at the sight of him, her undeniable pleasure marred by anger with Jack for taking it for granted he could just turn up any time he fancied without ringing first. She knew that he'd made a note of her number last Sunday. He'd been leaning on the counter right next to the phone. When the phone call never happened she assumed Jack had no interest in reviving their relationship and had resigned herself to the idea so determinedly that she resented him now, for coming back to unsettle her again.

'Would you like a drink?' she asked politely.

'Could I possibly have some tea?'

'Certainly. Sit down and take a look at the room while I make it.' Kate went off to the kitchen, thankful that she hadn't changed from the tailored black trousers and sweater of the afternoon. Strands of hair were escaping from its coil, and her face could have done with attention, but Jack looked too tired to notice. He was probably hungry too, if he'd driven from London. But he was out of luck if he expected a meal. A visitor was no part of her plan for the evening. She'd hung her new curtains, stood back to admire, and then eaten supper early so she could settle down in her finished sitting room to watch the gardening programme Jack had interrupted.

Kate returned with a tray and put it on a small Pembroke table between a pair of cane-sided Louis chairs cushioned in faded russet velvet.

'I like the room,' Jack told her, standing tall in the middle of it.

'Milk?' she asked, though she knew exactly how he liked his tea—or had done, once.

'Thank you.'

'Do sit down,' she said, handing him a cup. 'Try the modern chaise. It's better suited to someone your size than the chairs. They belonged to Aunt Edith,' she added, 'which is why they look so much at home here.'

He smiled a little. 'So do you, Kate.'

She nodded. 'Surprising, really. Until I was handed the key I hadn't been inside since I was a small child. My aunt leased it out to pay her way when she installed herself in a retirement home. I used to drive down from London once a month to see her. Aunt Edith was quite a character—a bit deaf, but with faculties in good shape otherwise right to the end. We got on well together, but when I was told she'd left her house to me I couldn't believe my luck. And the moment I set foot in here again it was love at first sight.'

'I remember it well.'

She frowned. 'You knew my aunt?'

'I'm referring to emotion, not property.' Jack looked her in the eye. 'For me it was love at first sight when I bought that poppy.'

Her stomach gave a lurch she covered with a hard little smile. 'It was for me, too. Such a shame that kind of thing doesn't last.'

His answering smile set her teeth on edge. 'How long was it for you, Kate? Until you got off the train in London?'

'No,' she said, pretending to think it over. 'Surely that was about the time you started sleeping with Dawn. It ended for me when I heard you'd married her.'

His face darkened. 'I've explained that.'

'So you have. You were lonely, she was willing and I'd gone. All the way to London—a mere two hour drive in that car of yours! I was devastated when you wouldn't even meet me to say goodbye, Jack,' she added with sudden heat. 'I know I was the one who actually ended it, but I still couldn't accept that it was over between us. I missed you so much I was ready to pack in my job and find work at home instead. I came back, just before Liz and Robert moved, to tell you that. And heard you'd married Dawn.'

Jack's mouth twisted. 'With hindsight I realise I was a quixotic fool, but at the time I felt I had no option. She swore her father would throw her out in the street when he found she was pregnant, and she had no money other than the small wage he paid her. So because the child could have been mine, I did the "decent thing",' he added with bitterness.

'Past history now.'

His eyes met hers. 'Only where Dawn's concerned; not for you and me, Kate. Have dinner with me tomorrow.'

Kate shook her head. 'Not a good idea, Jack.'

'Sunday, then.'

'I meant any night.'

He put down his cup and leaned forward, his long hands clasped loosely between his knees. 'What harm would there be in two old friends sharing a meal?'

'Because we were never just friends.'

'True,' he agreed. 'That very first time, after lunch at the pub—'

'The establishment run by Dawn Taylor's father.'

'That's the one. You thought you'd been shameless.'

Kate fondly believed she'd kicked the habit of blushing, but with Jack's eyes holding hers she felt the annoying warmth rising in her face. 'I thought I'd had a terrible nerve,' she corrected, and felt the colour deepen at his look of triumph.

'You remember! I had to fight to keep my hands off you.'

She thawed a little. 'Did you?'

Jack nodded. 'We had something very special, Kate.'

'I don't deny it,' she agreed soberly. 'But the past tense says it all. We're different people now, older and hopefully wiser. Enough to know we can't go back.'

He looked sceptical. 'You came back here to live. You knew you risked running into me again.'

She shook her head. 'No risk to me, Jack. I thought you

were married, remember, and father of several children for all I knew.'

'And now you know I'm neither?'

Kate thought about it. 'I suppose the odd dinner would be pleasant. But nothing more than that, Jack. Relationships are altogether too much work.'

He nodded in grim agreement. 'I gave up on them the day my divorce came through.'

'So what do you do for—' She paused. 'Feminine solace?'

'You mean sex?' he said bluntly. 'I steer clear locally. But I spend regular time in London these days. I've got a flat near my offices there.'

'You mean you pay for your pleasures?' she said, equally blunt.

He looked affronted. 'Hell, no. I've never needed to. Besides, I have strong objections to sharing in that context. I just want your company over dinner, Kate,' he added. 'No strings.'

'No feminine solace involved?' she said lightly.

'Just the pleasure of your company would give me that, Kate.'

She looked at him thoughtfully. He'd asked to see her again, just as she'd wanted. If she was going to turn him down flat, now was the time to do it. Instead she found herself nodding in agreement. 'Why not?'

'Good,' said Jack briskly, and stood up. 'I'll call for you tomorrow. Seven-thirty?'

'Make it eight.' Kate went to the door with him. 'It was good to see your father again.'

'Dad thinks you've matured into a very beautiful woman.'

'How sweet of him! I like your dog, by the way.'

'I'll bring Bran to visit one day.'

'Please do. I thought your father looked great, Jack.'

He nodded. 'I hope I look half as good at his age.'

'The resemblance is so strong you're bound to.' Kate

smiled up at him, and Jack bent and kissed her lightly on the cheek.

'See you tomorrow. Thanks for the tea.'

Jack Logan drove home in triumphant mood. So Kate was willing to settle for friendship. He could wait until she was ready for more. He'd felt her stiffen slightly as he kissed her cheek, as though she'd been afraid he meant to do more than that, so the wait was unlikely to be long. She could say what she liked about relationships, but the chemistry between them still existed, alive and kicking, even after all these years apart.

His mouth tightened. The long parting would never have happened if he hadn't been such an idiot about Dawn. He should have questioned his paternity, or just offered to pay child support. But when Kate Durant preferred a London career to marriage with Jack Logan it wasn't only his heart that suffered. So he took what Dawn offered to massage his ego, and then paid for the privilege in the way he knew would hurt Kate most. It was years later before he realised how hard his marriage must have hit her when he heard that she was living with some banker in a pricey Dockside loft. But that was in the past. Now the banker was long gone, and so was the successor she wouldn't talk about. Jack Logan had developed patience over the years, and Katherine Durant was a woman worth waiting for.

Alone in her sitting room, Kate sat staring into space, sure she'd made a big mistake. Jack had finally asked to see her again and, instead of turning him down flat, she'd heard herself agreeing—just as she'd done the first time. But she had to eat. And it was only dinner, no bed and breakfast involved. Surely they could be friends again. Not that there was any 'again' about it. They'd never been just friends.

That first night in the cinema they'd sat together without even holding hands, yet by the time he'd stopped the car on the way home she'd been desperate for his kisses and anything else Jack Logan had to offer. She'd never been keen on the physical side of relationships up to that point, and frustrated, angry boyfriends had never stayed the course very long. With Jack it was so different she'd felt as though she'd die if he didn't take her to bed. And when he did she thought she'd died anyway, and gone to heaven. She smiled wistfully at the memory. Because they'd both lived at home with relatives the opportunities to repeat the experience had not been plentiful. But when either Tom Logan or the Suttons went out for the evening they'd dived into Jack's bed or hers the moment they were alone together.

That particular form of high-octane rapture happened only once apparently. She had never experienced it again.

When Jack Logan came for her, formal-suited and prompt at eight the following evening, Kate was ready in clinging wool crêpe the colour of vintage cognac. Long-sleeved and starkly plain, the dress relied on superb fit and a vertiginous neckline for its impact. And Jack's face told Kate that the dress, by no means new, was still worth every penny of the outrageous price she'd once paid for it.

'You look wonderful,' he told her.

Resisting the urge to tell him he did too, she thanked him politely. 'Would you like a drink before we go?'

'I'll wait until we get there.' Jack held her long black trench coat for her, and looked on in approval while she set her alarm and locked her door. 'I'm glad to see you're safety conscious.'

'Big city habits.' She smiled, impressed, when Jack opened the passenger door of his car. 'A Jensen, no less!'

'Classic cars are my hobby these days,' he told her, as he slid behind the wheel, 'and in common with Bran, a lot less trouble than humans.'

Kate laughed. 'You mean women.'

'If the cap fits,' he agreed, eyes crinkling.

Instead of making for the town centre as she'd expected,

Jack drove in the opposite direction. 'Country pub?' she asked.

'I've organised dinner at home. I thought you'd like to see my house.'

He was right about that! 'The one no woman sets foot in?' she asked lightly.

'Molly Carter sets foot in it regularly, twice a week when I'm away, more when I'm not.'

'I came across pictures of it in a magazine once, with a big article about you,' she told him, remembering her shock at finding his face in her Sunday paper. 'My colleagues were deeply impressed when I mentioned—very casually—that I knew you.'

'Did you say how well?'

'No. Not even Anna knew that.' She hesitated, then asked something she'd been burning to ask for years. 'Jack, did you pass your mother's ring on to Dawn?'

'No,' he said shortly, and turned down a narrow road towards a pair of handsome, wrought-iron gates. 'These are original,' he told her as he aimed a remote control.

Kate sat tense in anticipation as the car moved slowly along a narrow drive lined with trees. At the end of it Jack circled round a lawn to park in front of a long house with light blazing from rows of tall windows.

'Two hundred years ago it was a flax mill, but when I came on the scene it was practically a ruin,' Jack told her. 'At first I thought it was too far gone for restoration.'

'But you could see what it would become,' said Kate with respect. 'Or what it could go back to.'

'Exactly,' he said with satisfaction. As she got out of the car Kate's eyes lit up at the sight of a familiar figure in the open doorway.

'Tom!' she said in delight.

'I thought you wouldn't mind an extra guest, Kate,' said Jack dryly.

Tom Logan kissed her affectionately. 'I said he was mad to want his father along when he'd asked a beautiful woman to dinner, but Jack insisted.'

'Quite right, too,' she assured him, fleeting disappointment replaced by relief. Jack was obviously *not* expecting feminine solace in return for dinner.

CHAPTER FOUR

'WELCOME to my humble abode,' said Jack, the mockery in his smile telling Kate her relief was written on her face. 'I'll take your coat.'

'I'll do that,' said his father. 'You show her the house.'

Kate had pored greedily over the photographs in the magazine article but seeing the house with her own eyes was a different experience. A faded Persian carpet softened the granite flags of the entrance hall, but the main impression was light. The crystal-strung candles of twin chandeliers poured light down on walls and banisters painted pristine white. Kate stood utterly still for a moment then crossed the hall, drawn by the only painting on view, a portrait of a handsome, rakish man in Regency dress over a fireplace obviously original to the building.

'How very grand. He wasn't in the photographs. Is he an ancestor?' she asked, and Jack shook his head, grinning.

'Dad thought the chap looked a bit like me, so he bought it at auction.'

Jack led her across the hall into a long room with more white walls and rows of tall windows, but the light was softer here, from lamps shaded in neutral silk. An antique desk lived in harmony with large-scale modern furniture, but it was the dimension of the room that silenced Kate.

'Say something!' urged Jack.

'It's breathtaking. All this space!' She smiled as she waved a hand at the windows. 'You've got something against curtains?'

He shrugged. 'No neighbours, and the windows are draught-proof, made to my own specification to blend with the house. I had some blinds made for the bedrooms, but otherwise I let in as much light as possible.'

Kate gazed round her in awe. 'The photographs didn't do it justice. My place is a doll's house by comparison.'

'But equally attractive in its own way.' He took her arm. 'Let's join Dad. It's time I gave you a drink.'

The entire evening proved far more relaxed for Kate with Tom Logan there than if she'd spent it alone with Jack. The food was simple—a casserole of fork-tender beef slow-cooked with vegetables, herbs and wine and eaten at the kitchen table, with Bran casting a hopeful eye on the proceedings from his bed.

'It's cosier in here for just three of us.' Tom smiled affectionately at Kate. 'And it's not the first time we've eaten together round a kitchen table.'

'No, indeed. I used to love meals at your house.' She pulled a face. 'There was more formality at ours. My sister brought out the best china if Jack so much as ate a sandwich with us.'

'Which wasn't that often,' Jack reminded her caustically. 'Our relationship was cut painfully short.'

'Now then,' said his father sternly. 'You can't ask a girl to dinner, then throw the past in her face. You're not on firm ground there yourself.'

'How very true.' Jack gave Kate an ironic bow as he got up to take her plate. 'My apologies. How about organic ice cream straight from Addison's farm shop?'

'Perfect,' she said lightly.

After the meal Tom Logan took Kate into the living room while Jack made coffee. 'So, what do you think of the house that Jack built?' he asked as he put logs on the fire.

'Impressive,' she told him, gazing round the room. 'It's nothing like my preconceived idea of a mill house, much more of a home. But very definitely a man's home. Other than that muscular bit of sculpture on the desk, there are no ornaments, no photographs—just one solitary landscape and the art deco mirror over the fireplace.'

'It needs a woman's touch,' said Tom slyly, and laughed at the look she gave him. 'Just teasing!'

She grinned. 'I can just picture Jack's face if I suggested cushions and a flower arrangement.'

'I heard that,' said Jack, coming in with a tray. He set it down on the massive slab of rosewood used as a coffee table. 'You find my taste austere?'

'It suits the house.'

'Which doesn't answer my question.'

She began pouring coffee. 'My opinion doesn't matter. You're the one who lives here.' She smiled at him as he added a sugar lump to his father's cup. 'But actually I like your house very much, Jack.'

'It's a big place for one man,' observed Tom Logan, and looked round as Bran padded into the room. 'Is he allowed in here tonight?'

'Of course he is.' Jack bent to fondle the dog's head. 'I give him the run of the ground floor when I'm at home, but upstairs it's permanently off limits. To dogs, anyway,' he added, as Bran stretched out in front of the fire.

'Who cooked the dinner?' asked Kate. 'You, Jack?'

'Molly made it this morning, and I followed her instructions and put it in a slow oven at the required time.' He took a cup from the tray and sat down on the chair nearest to Kate's corner of the sofa. 'I forgot to ask if your tastes in food had changed.'

'What would you have done if I was a vegetarian these days? Opened a tin of baked beans?'

'We often shared one in the old days.'

Kate gave him a serene smile. 'But these are new days, Jack.' She turned to his father. 'Are you playing golf tomorrow, Tom?'

For the rest of the evening Jack was the perfect host. He

gave up sniping about the past, and even suggested that Kate came back to see the place in daylight one day and eat lunch on the terrace overlooking the mill pond. 'I keep a small boat if you fancy a row some time. It's a healthy way to keep fit.'

'Sounds good,' said Kate enviously. 'My rare bouts of exercise are in a gym. Rowing on water in fresh air sounds a lot more tempting.'

'Bring your niece in the school holidays,' said Jack. 'The garden in Park Crescent can't be very big. You could give her the run of the grounds here.'

'Poor little thing,' said Tom with compassion. 'It's been a big upheaval for her. How's she coping?'

Kate's eyes shadowed. 'Christmas was tricky—the first without her parents.'

'Did she come to you in London for it?' asked Jack.

Kate shook her head. 'Apart from a brief stay with her grandparents, Joanna spent the entire Christmas break in the Maitland household with me. Both sets of parents were there and neighbours came in for drinks, so there was a lot going on. One couple brought twin teenage sons along as company for Jo and she got on well with them, and spent quite a lot of time with them over the holiday. I took her shopping for furniture for her new bedroom, and we spent hours poring over paint charts together—everything I could think of to keep her in the loop over the move to Park Crescent. But neither of us enjoyed the day she went back to school,' she added bleakly.

'Half term can't be far away,' said Jack with sympathy, but she shook her head.

'There isn't one this term. Her school goes for the longer Easter holiday. But I'll drive down to take her out for lunch before then.'

Soon afterwards Tom Logan got up to go.

'You can't leave now, Dad,' protested his son.

'Early round of golf in the morning. Must get my beauty sleep.'

Kate got to her feet. 'Then maybe you'd give me a lift, Mr Logan. You pass near my place.'

'Don't go yet, Kate.' Jack put a hand on her arm.

'No, indeed. You stay, my dear,' said his father, kissing her cheek. 'Otherwise I'll feel guilty. Jack will run you home later.'

When Jack came back with the dog, Kate turned from the study of tree-fringed water in his painting. 'Where is this?'

'Right here in the grounds. It's the mill pond, complete with willows and chestnut trees.'

'You commissioned it?'

He nodded. 'Local artist. I was impressed by an exhibition of her work. She agreed to do it once she'd approved the location.'

'Would she have turned you down if she hadn't?'

'More than likely. But she took one look and named her price—which was steep. But I paid it willingly when I saw the finished work.'

Kate turned away, smiling wryly. 'How things have changed. When we were together I was just earning peanuts and you weren't much better off.'

'At the time Dad and I were ploughing most of the profits back into the business.' He bent to poke the fire. 'If he hadn't handed my mother's ring over I certainly couldn't have bought one for you right then. I had to borrow money from him for Dawn's settlement.'

Controlling her reaction to Dawn's name, Kate smiled brightly at Jack. 'But nowadays Logan Development is a roaring success and you can buy what you like.'

He straightened, and gave her a look which almost had her backing away. 'Is that your benchmark of success, Kate? To be able to buy what you like?'

Her eyes narrowed coldly. 'If it were would I have turned my back on a highly paid job?'

'I thought you did that to take care of your niece.'

'If it had been absolutely vital I kept the job Joanna could have shared my flat in Notting Hill, and I would have paid someone to look after her in the school holidays. But to me it seemed far more important to make a home for her here and look after her myself.'

'And you're right, Kate,' he said, with contrition. 'You obviously care very deeply for Joanna. I don't have a child in my life—one of the many things money can't buy.'

She turned away, looking at her watch. 'I should be going soon.'

'Why? I thought the great advantage of the new job was its flexibility.'

'I'm making a start on my bedroom. I'm sleeping in Jo's for the time being.'

'But there's time for a nightcap before you go, Kate. It's early,' he added, 'and you haven't seen the rest of the house.'

'I'll have some fruit juice, if you like, but I'll leave the rest of the tour, Jack.' The last thing she wanted at this stage was a visit to his bedroom, much as she'd like to see it. He might talk about being friends, but it wasn't easy. He'd been her lover for a brief, ecstatic time when they were young, but there had been long years after that when she'd thought of Jack Logan with no love at all.

'Sit down again,' said Jack. 'I'll bring your drink.'

Kate bent to fondle Bran instead. The dog half-closed his eyes in ecstasy as she found exactly the right spot behind his ear.

'You're a very handsome fellow,' she told him. 'I always wanted a dog like you.'

'You weren't allowed to have one?' asked Jack, and handed her a glass.

Kate shook her head. 'Elizabeth wouldn't allow it, and her

word was law. As you know, my mother died when I was born, and my father when I was ten, not long after Elizabeth got married. So Liz and Robert seemed like parents to me—and pretty strict ones at that. But it was good of them to take care of me,' she added hastily.

'You're repaying them by taking care of Joanna?'

'Absolutely not. I'm doing it because I love her.' She shivered. 'Let's talk about something else.'

'Come and sit down.' He switched off two of the lamps, stirred the fire into life and led her to the sofa. 'I never thought this would happen,' he said, sitting beside her.

Kate made no pretence of misunderstanding. 'You mean the two of us together like this in your amazing house?'

'Exactly.' Jack turned to smile at her, a glint in his eyes that had turned her knees to jelly when she was twenty.

But she wasn't twenty any more. 'I know what you mean. When I found those pictures in the magazine, I never imagined I'd see the place for myself.'

'It must have been quite a surprise to come across my face in your Sunday paper.'

Surprise didn't begin to cover it. 'Yes,' she said dryly, 'it certainly was.'

'Were you between fiancés at the time?'

'You sound as though I had a string of them!' she said tartly, and sipped some of her drink. 'I happened to be alone that morning, but I showed the article to Rupert later and mentioned that I knew you. I searched the piece for personal details about you, but the emphasis was on your professional life.'

'That was the deal with the journalist.'

Kate turned to look at him. 'Jack, where did you live when you were married?'

His eyes shuttered. 'Dad suggested we move into the block of flats the company was renovating on Gloucester Road at the time. I tried to make a go of the marriage, but Dawn and

I had so little in common it was obvious from the start that it was never going to work.' He drained his glass and turned to look at her. 'It's a part of my life I look back on with no pleasure at all—or pride.'

'You fulfilled your obligations, Jack.'

'But I did so for the wrong reasons,' he said savagely. 'I wanted to hurt you as much as I wanted to do the right thing for Dawn.'

She nodded sadly. 'You succeeded on both counts.'

'And soon realised my colossal mistake.' He was silent for a long interval, his eyes sombre as he stared into the fire. 'The surprise came when I learned that the baby wasn't mine. I found I'd actually wanted a child. My child, anyway. Does that sound mad to you?'

She shook her head mutely.

He smoothed his thumb over the back of her hand in silence for a while. 'So tell me,' he said, turning to look at her. 'Why did you send the third man packing? Was he another one wanting babies and a place in the country?'

'No. He didn't want children at all.' Her eyes kindled. 'I broke up with Rupert because he refused to take Joanna as part of the deal.'

Jack stared at her. 'What the devil did he expect you to do with her?'

'Hand her over to Robert's parents, who are lovely people, but far too elderly and frail to cope with a child of her age on a permanent basis. When I explained this he gave me an ultimatum. I had to choose between the child and him, right then and there. So I made it brutally clear that there was no question of choice, and never would be.' Her mouth tightened. 'Rupert took it badly—very badly.'

His fingers tightened on her hand. 'What happened?'

Kate eyes glittered icily at the thought of it. 'He flew into such a rage I thought he was going to beat me up. Dr Jekyll turned into Mr Hyde right there in front of me. But I was too furious on Jo's behalf to feel afraid. I just stood there, eye to eye, daring him to hit me. It was touch and go for a while, but like all bullies Rupert backed down in the end. At which point I threw the ring at him and told him to get out of my life.'

'Good God!' Jack stared at her, appalled. 'You took a hell of a risk, Kate.'

'I realised that the moment he'd gone. I shook in my shoes for ages afterwards.' She turned to look at him. 'Now you can see why I hate talking about it. I just can't believe I was such a bad judge of character.'

'Not entirely,' he reminded her. 'Instinct warned you not to move in with him.'

'True.' Kate's eyes darkened. 'He was in such a rush about everything, I felt uneasy. He bought the ring just days after our first meeting, but no matter how much he argued I insisted we had to know each other better before I actually wore it.'

'Did you love him?'

'I was attracted to him, certainly. He was charming, witty and very good company. But until that horrible night I'd never come up against the real Rupert Chance.' She shrugged. 'It clinched my decision to give up my job. I'd worked in Personnel for years and prided myself on my judgement when it came to people. If that was no longer working for me it was time to call it a day.'

'Did Joanna like him?'

'She never met him. He was abroad at the time of the funeral. My relationship with Rupert—if you could call it that—lasted less than a school term. Why?'

'Her reaction to him might have been interesting.' Jack gave her a crooked smile. 'I get a card from Sydney every Christmas, with the current snapshot of Dawn, husband and progeny—three sons at the last count. Her way of telling me she's a respectable matron these days.'

'Is she still gorgeous?' asked Kate, hoping Dawn had lost her looks by now.

'In a different, earth-mother kind of way I suppose she is.' Jack shrugged. 'She looks contented with her life, and who can ask more than that?'

'Are you contented with yours?'

He was silent for a moment, his eyes on the fire. 'I'm head of a very successful outfit,' he said slowly, 'with a beautiful house here and a flat in London, and I'm the proud owner of several classic cars and a great dog. So I must be contented.' He turned to look at her. 'Are you?'

'Yes,' said Kate firmly. 'I'm going to make a good life here for Joanna.'

'She's fortunate to have you to care for her.'

She shook her head. 'It's my good fortune to have Jo.'

'I'd like to meet her some time. You don't like the idea?' he added as she frowned.

'It's more a case of whether Jo likes it. I'd have to ask her first.'

Jack got up, clicking his fingers to the dog, who padded after him obediently. 'I'll just put him out for a moment.'

Kate sat very still when she was alone, staring, unseeing, into the fire.

'You're still frowning,' said Jack, coming back into the room.

Kate managed a smile. 'Just thinking. Where's Bran?'

'In bed.'

'Sensible chap. I should be making tracks for my own bed soon.'

'First tell me what's making you look so blue, Katie.'

Damn. She'd always turned to marshmallow when he called her that. 'You want the truth?'

He smiled crookedly. 'Probably not, but I promise I'll take it like a man.'

'To revert to the friendship issue—'

'You've changed your mind?' Jack sat down beside her and took her hand.

'No.'

'But you're thinking of Joanna. You chose her without hesitation over the objectionable Rufus—'

'Rupert.'

'Right. So it was obvious you'd make the same choice if she objected to me.'

'Exactly.' Kate smiled ruefully. 'So if I'm too much work as a friend I'll understand, Jack.'

'I've never been afraid of work.'

'I know that. Your father is very proud of you.'

His eyes softened. 'The funny thing is, Kate, that if you'd stayed with me I might not have achieved the same level of success. The all out concentration would have been impossible with you around to distract me.'

'Then maybe I did you a good turn by running off.'

'It didn't feel like it at the time,' he retorted.

'Nor to me.' Kate shook her head in wonder. 'I was such a *girl* when I met you, Jack. But I grew up pretty quickly after you dumped me.'

His eyes glittered dangerously. 'Your memory's at fault, Katherine Durant. It was you who dumped me.'

'Only technically!' She glared back. 'I had to salvage some remnant of pride! You wouldn't even meet me to say goodbye.'

'I was afraid I'd go down on my knees and beg you to stay.'

They stared at each other in silence broken suddenly by a log falling in the fireplace.

'That's an unlikely picture,' said Kate at last.

'The knees maybe,' he conceded. 'But not the begging.'

She shook her head. 'I can't imagine it.'

He shrugged. 'It belongs in the past, anyway, Kate. Far better to focus on the present.'

'You're right about that,' she said with a sigh. 'When Liz and Robert were killed, my own mortality hit me in the face. I even made a will.'

'Good move. Thinking in worst scenario terms,' he added, 'what provision is made for Joanna if anything happens to you, Kate?'

'Guardianship would go to her Sutton grandparents, with Anna and Ben named in the will as trustees.' She yawned suddenly. 'Sorry. It must be this fire. I really must go home now, Jack. Sorry to drag you out.'

He got up at once, and held out his hand to help her up. 'A gentleman—even the self-made variety like me—always sees a lady home, Miss Durant.'

'Another time I'll bring my car,' she told him, and flushed as she heard the promise implicit in her words. 'I'll just say goodnight to Bran before we go,' she said hastily.

'I hit on a good idea by asking Dad along,' said Jack on the drive back. 'You relaxed the moment you saw him, so you were obviously worried when I took you to my place for dinner.' He shot her a sidelong glance. 'Were you afraid that I'd fall on you with ravening lust before the meal or after it?'

Kate let out a snort of laughter. 'Neither, Jack. But you're right about your father. It was an inspired move to ask him along.'

'The idea was to convince you that my intentions were strictly honourable!'

'It succeeded. I enjoyed the evening very much.'

'In that case, come again soon.'

'The two of you must come to me next time,' she said impulsively, then bit her lip. 'But I'll have to paint my dining room first. Otherwise it's the kitchen table again.'

'As Dad said, it's something we've done often enough before.' Jack gave her a searching look as he parked outside her house. 'Tell me, Kate. Why are you doing all the painting yourself? Cash flow problem?'

Kate shook her head. 'It's just my way of putting my personal mark on the house—making it really mine.' She hesitated. 'Would you like some coffee?'

She unlocked her door and Jack followed her through the brightly lit house to the kitchen. He helped her off with her coat then turned her round into his arms.

'No coffee, not even ravening lust. Just this, Katie.' He bent his head and kissed her, and for a moment she stood ramrod stiff, fighting her own response. But as the kiss deepened, her lips parted to the irresistible familiarity and sheer rightness of it. With a sigh she surrendered to the arms which tightened round her, all her senses urging her to taste him, touch him, drink in the male, remembered scent of him as her body responded to the mounting urgency in his. *No,* reminded a voice in her head and she took in a sharp, shaky breath and pulled free. Jack raised his head and stepped back, eyes gleaming under narrowed lids.

'When a gentleman sees a lady home he deserves a goodnight kiss.'

She smiled brightly. 'What's a kiss between friends?'

'Do you kiss all your friends like that?'

'Only the men!'

Jack laughed. 'The girl I knew would have blushed when she said that.'

Kate shrugged. 'That girl grew up fast, Jack.'

'And I'm to blame.'

'Mostly,' she agreed, and went with him to the door.

'I must try to make amends. But before I leave I want something else.' He grinned as she backed away. 'Don't panic—just your mobile phone number.' He noted the number in his diary, then tore out a page, scribbled his own number and handed it over. 'Right then, Kate. If you need me, ring me any time. Goodnight.' Jack kissed her cheek and crossed the pavement to his car.

*   *   *

Mill House was the main topic of conversation over Sunday lunch next day at the Maitland house. Ben was as interested in Kate's description of the actual property as his wife, but he hooted at the look on Anna's face when she heard that Tom Logan had been present.

'Didn't Jack trust himself alone with you?' she demanded.

'Of course he did. But when the past rears its head between us the atmosphere tends to get a little tense. With Mr Logan there as peace-keeper it was a very pleasant evening.'

Anna sighed in disappointment. 'No red-hot sex then?'

'For God's sake, wife,' said her husband, laughing. 'You can't ask questions like that.'

Kate rolled her eyes. 'Oh, yes, she can, and frequently does. But, to satisfy your curiosity, Mrs Maitland, I made it very clear to Jack that the only thing on offer is friendship.'

'He was *happy* with that?' said Ben sceptically.

'He appears to be.'

'So when are you seeing him again?' asked Anna.

'We haven't set a date. But it's up to me, anyway. I'm giving Jack—and his father—supper at my place next time.'

'Is this going to be a regular kind of thing, then?'

'I hope so. I'm very fond of Mr Logan.'

Anna hooted. 'And what about Mr Logan Junior? How do you feel about him?'

'Ambivalent.' Kate smiled suddenly. 'Before I left London people kept asking me what on earth I'd find to do up here in the sticks. Time certainly hasn't hung heavy so far.'

CHAPTER FIVE

IN CONFIRMATION of this a message was waiting on Kate's telephone when she got home that evening.

'Richard Forster here, Kate. If you're an Oscar Wilde fan *The Importance of Being Earnest* is on at the Playhouse this week. I can get tickets for Wednesday or Thursday if you'd like to see it. We could eat somewhere first—or after. Let me know.'

When Kate rang him Richard sounded so delighted to hear from her she wouldn't have had the heart to say no even if she'd wanted to. Friendship with Jack Logan, she reminded herself stringently, needn't exclude all other men from her life.

'I love Oscar Wilde,' she told him. 'Thursday would be good. How are you?'

They chatted together for a while, arranged times and discussed eating places for their evening out, and Kate rang off at last, feeling rather pleased with life. Her good mood lasted for all of fifteen minutes, until Jack rang.

'You're hard to find,' he said irritably. 'You were out this morning, the line was engaged just now—and you've had your mobile switched off all day.'

'And hello to you, too.'

'Where were you?'

'Out,' she said baldly.

'I gathered that. I went for a run in the park with Bran and called at your house afterwards.'

'Apologise to Bran for me.'

'I told you I'd call in next time.'

'Surely you don't expect me to hang around on the off

63

chance! Anyway, now you're on the line it saves writing to thank you for last night.'

'The kiss was thanks enough,' said Jack, in a tone that curled her toes. 'Look, I'm tied up the first half of the week, but how about dinner on Thursday?'

'Sorry,' she said sweetly. 'I'm going to the theatre that night.'

'Pity,' he said, after a pause. 'Another time, then.'

'Lovely. Goodnight, Jack—'

'Hold it. Where were you today, Kate?'

She ground her teeth. 'Sunday lunch with the Maitlands. Satisfied now?'

'Not by any means. Goodnight.'

A slow smile spread across Kate's face as he disconnected. How lucky that Richard had asked her out first. Otherwise she might have been tempted to say yes to Jack. Instead he could just wait until she invited him to supper with his father. She liked Richard Forster's restful, unthreatening brand of charm, whereas there was something about Jack these days that made her uneasy. Not just the kiss last night, though that had been scary enough, if only because it made her crave more of the same. But she had a feeling that deep down, offers of friendship or not, he had some kind of hidden agenda. Kate's eyes narrowed darkly. If there were any grudges to be harboured she had far more right to them than Jack. She'd been so young and trusting back then. She'd never dreamed that he would refuse to see her again after she left for London. She'd fondly believed that they'd kiss and make up once she made the first overture. She kept on believing it—right up to the day she heard Jack had married Dawn Taylor.

The next few days were fully occupied. Kate got up early each morning to work on her computer, and in the afternoons went on with her decorating. By Thursday the evening with Richard Forster was a welcome change from wielding a paint roller. The acting was good and the small theatre full, and afterwards they discussed the play over supper at a new restaurant near the Guildhall.

'So how are you settling in?' asked Richard later, over coffee Kate had asked for very deliberately so he wouldn't expect any when he drove her home.

'I've just finished painting my bedroom. Tomorrow the new mattress arrives and with luck I'll have the room ready to sleep in by bedtime.' She smiled cheerfully. 'After that it's one more room to go, and then I start on the garden.'

'Do you like gardening?'

'I used to when I was growing up here, but I haven't done any for years. I've been watching TV gardening programmes lately to pick up tips.'

'You might want to find someone to do the rough work if the garden's been neglected,' advised Richard.

'It's been kept in pretty good nick, fortunately, and it's not big. I can easily manage it myself. I've invested in some spanking new garden tools, so once the weather gets warmer I'll make a start.'

On the journey back to Park Crescent Richard asked if Kate was free for dinner on Saturday, but she shook her head.

'Sorry. I'm off to the Cotswolds for the weekend to see my niece.'

'Some other time then. Enjoy your trip. I'll give you a ring when you get back.'

To Kate's relief Richard stayed in the car when they reached the house. 'I'll wait until you're safe inside,' he said, smiling.

Kate smiled back warmly, grateful to him for making it clear he didn't expect to be asked in. 'Thanks again, Richard. Goodnight.'

Kate felt very thoughtful as she locked up. Richard's request to see her again was rather worrying. She had no intention of seeing anyone on a regular basis right now, least of all a man she suspected of pining for his wife. Frowning abstractedly, she checked her messages and found a very short one from Jack.

'I hope you enjoyed the play, Katie.'

She pressed the replay button, sure she must have missed something, but the electronic voice said, 'End of message.'

Kate went to bed in pensive mood, wondering, not for the first time lately, whether she would have moved back here if she'd known about Jack's divorce. But it was done now. Jo loved it here, and Kate had Anna and Ben for support if—if what? If friendship with Jack Logan proved to be the slightest threat to her life with Jo, she would simply dispense with it.

Kate left town at mid morning the following Saturday and after a leisurely drive arrived at her Cotswold hotel in time to settle in and change her clothes. She ordered a lavish tea for later then set off in good time to have a word with the headmistress before collecting Jo at Manor House School, which was a typical Cotswold structure in honeyed stone with the steep-pitched roof and mullioned windows common to local architecture.

Kate was conducted straight to the headmistress's office, and once the greetings were over Dr Knight gave her the information she was anxious to hear.

'Joanna has done remarkably well since her return this term, Miss Durant. She is a mature child, and is coping bravely with her personal tragedy. There may well be tears when she's alone, but I have emphasized that she can come to me, or to Miss Hayes, my deputy, at any time. And Matron keeps a close eye on her, of course.'

'Thank you,' said Kate gratefully. 'It was very hard to part with her when I brought her back at the beginning of term. But during our weekly phone call she seems to be coping.'

'She's doing well, I assure you. And, in confidence,' added Dr Knight, 'Joanna told me she is very happy to be making her home with you, Miss Durant. She tells me you inherited a house.'

Kate gave a few details about it, then got up to leave. 'Thank you for seeing me, Dr Knight.'

The headmistress smiled as she shook hands. 'I'm always available if you have concerns. In the meantime, if you go down to the main hall and sign the book, Joanna will be there in a few minutes.'

Kate went downstairs to join a crowd of people on the same mission, and soon afterwards a bell rang and teachers ushered a stream of girls of various ages through the double doors.

Jo's bright hair was easy to spot among the tide of grey tweed overcoats. She said a word to a teacher, then came hurrying through the crowd, and Kate hugged her close for an instant.

'Love the pinstripes!' Jo cast approving dark eyes over Kate's trouser suit.

'Must get some mileage out of my old work clothes. I've signed the book. Should I be checking you out with someone?'

'I've already done that. Miss Hayes says I must be back by half past six.'

'Let's go, then.' They made their way through the chattering mêlée of girls and parents and went out to the car. 'I thought we'd have tea at my hotel,' said Kate as they drove off. 'Either in the lounge there, or you can sprawl on the bed in my room and watch television while you pig out on sandwiches and cake.'

'Guess which I prefer!' said Jo, with a giggle which did Kate's heart good.

'So how are you, Miss Niece?' she asked bluntly.

Jo sobered. 'I'm OK, sort of. I still have bad times, but not so often now.'

'Are they at night?'

'Sometimes. But the mornings are the worst when I wake up and realise I'll never see Mum and Dad any more.'

Kate swallowed a lump in her throat, unable to speak for a moment.

'I get over it by thinking of something else,' went on Joanna. 'You and the new house, Anna and Ben, even Josh and Leo, the terrible twins. Or I concentrate on a maths test or the prep I've got to get through later.' She straightened in her seat. 'Mummy wouldn't want me to be crying all the time.'

Listening in awe, Kate had to remind herself that Jo was only thirteen. 'You're absolutely right, darling. So what social events are delighting you this term?'

'There's a disco next Saturday night. Just girls, though.'

'I thought you socialised with the boys from King Edward's occasionally.'

'Not in the junior school, worse luck,' said Jo, pulling a face. 'Was it the same with you?'

'I went to an ordinary co-ed day school, with boys around all the time. At your age I was more interested in hockey and netball than any of that lot.'

Jo cast a mischievous glance at Kate's face. 'How about right now? Have you met anyone since you moved back home?'

'Yes,' said Kate with perfect truth. 'Lots of people. I told you about Anna's party, but since then I've had dinner with an old friend and I've been to the theatre with a new one. And here's some stop press news. Anna's going to have a baby!'

This information diverted Jo so effectively from Kate's social life that she talked of nothing else until they reached the hotel. Kate collected her key and asked to have tea sent up as soon as possible, then took Jo upstairs to a pleasant double room overlooking the grounds at the back of the building.

'Cool,' said Jo, impressed. 'Can I watch television?'

'You can do anything you like—within reason!'

Jo went off to explore the bathroom, exclaiming about the various products provided by the hotel, then came back to prop herself up on the bed and spend a happy few minutes with the remote control before finding a channel with a re-run of *Grease*.

'This is brilliant,' she said with smile of satisfaction. 'Can we have lunch here tomorrow, too?'

'If you like. Or would you prefer a scenic drive and a country pub somewhere?'

The smile faded. 'No, thank you. I'd rather come back here.'

Kate could have kicked herself. No child would fancy driving far after losing her parents in a road accident. 'Good choice. The receptionist told me they do a very good Sunday lunch here.'

Jo brightened. 'It's sure to beat school dinners!'

When a waiter arrived to deposit a laden tray on the small table Kate sent him on his way with a generous tip and pulled up two basket chairs. 'Right, then. Let's see what they found for us.'

Jo gazed in delight at the array of sandwiches, crumpets, cakes and scones, and two bowls of fresh fruit salad.

'Wow!' she said, and shook out a napkin to protect her grey uniform skirt. 'May I start?'

Using dinner later as her excuse, Kate ate very little, content just to drink tea and enjoy Jo's account of tests she'd done well in and others she hadn't, of goals she'd scored in netball, the dance session with her friends in front of *Top of the Pops* on television on Friday nights, and the wild, but much admired, exploits of Giles, the brother of her friend, Emma.

'How old is he?'

'Oh, quite old. He's in his first year at university.'

'That old!'

Jo grinned as she spread cream and jam on a scone. 'Jane's got a brother, too, but he's only fifteen.' She sighed. 'I would have liked a brother—or a sister.'

Kate's heart contracted. She put out a hand to touch a rather sticky little paw. 'I'm sure Anna will let you have a share in the baby.'

Jo's eyes lit up at the thought. 'I wonder what she'll have. Will Anna have a scan to find out?'

'I'll ask when I get home.'

After driving Jo back to school Kate felt at rather a loose end when she returned to the hotel. To pass the time until dinner she had a shower, fiddled a lot with her hair afterwards, and then rang Anna for a chat.

'Hi, Mumsie. How are you?'

'At this time of day fine. You do not, however, want anything to do with me in the mornings. How's Jo?'

'Doing well, thank God. She assures me she's coping and her headmistress confirmed it.'

'She's got grit, that niece of yours. Did you tell her about the baby?'

'Of course I did. She was thrilled to bits. She asked if you're going to find out what sex it is.'

'Good heavens no! Give her my love tomorrow, but say we'd rather wait until the baby's born. Oh, by the way— breaking news. Jack Logan has invited the Maitlands to dinner at Mill House next weekend. I trust you're suitably impressed.'

Kate blinked. 'I certainly am. Enormously. Is this pay back for gatecrashing your party?'

'Must be. Lucy will be livid.' Anna gave a little cough. 'Has he asked you, too?'

'No. The honour's all yours.'

'He only rang today. Maybe there'll be a message waiting for you when you get back. And report in the minute you arrive, please; the weather forecast's not great.'

Kate went down to the crowded, noisy bar in thoughtful mood. She ordered a glass of wine and sat down at the solitary vacant table to study the menu.

'The other tables are full. Would you mind if I shared?' said a pleasant male voice, and Kate looked up to see a man who looked vaguely familiar.

'Of course not. Do sit down.'

'I saw you at Manor House School this afternoon,' he said as he took the seat opposite. 'I'm Philip Brace. My daughter Leah is a pupil there.'

Kate smiled, enlightened. 'Ah, I see. I'm Kate Durant. I'm visiting my niece, Joanna Sutton.'

'In that case could I persuade you to join forces with me for dinner?' He gave her a rueful grin. 'I'd be grateful for company.'

'Was your wife unable to come?' asked Kate pointedly.

The smile vanished. 'We're recently divorced—very recently. It's my first turn to take Leah out this weekend.'

'Oh, I see,' said Kate, wishing she'd kept her mouth shut.

Philip Brace looked at her levelly. 'I can leave you in peace if you prefer.'

'Not at all. I'd be glad of company, too. Have you driven far?'

Having established that they lived less than thirty miles from each other, they discussed Jo and Leah, and exchanged opinions on the education the girls were receiving before breaking off to give their orders to the hovering waiter.

'I would have felt conspicuous as the only person on my own,' Kate admitted, once they were seated in the formal dining room later.

'I get more than enough of it on my travels for the firm.' He smiled hopefully. 'I'm driving Leah to Chipping Camden for lunch tomorrow. Would you and Jo care to join us?'

Kate explained about the tragedy which had turned Jo

against car journeys, and said something polite about joining forces some other time.

Philip shot her a look as he poured the wine he'd ordered. 'If I get too pushy just tell me to back off.'

'Oh, I will,' she assured him, smiling to take the edge off her words.

'One question,' he went on, once their first course was in front of them. 'If you are Jo's aunt, is there a matching uncle?'

'No. Other than me, her only relatives are a pair of elderly grandparents.'

'Poor little thing!' He smiled wryly. 'As you can probably tell, I was trying to find out whether I was trespassing on someone's preserves.'

'If you were I would have said no,' she assured him, and got on with her excellent dinner. The meal passed very pleasantly, they opted for coffee at the table afterwards, but when they left the dining room Kate stopped at the foot of the main staircase in the hall and held out her hand.

'I'll say goodnight now, Philip.'

'Shall I see you at breakfast in the morning?'

She shook her head smiling. 'I'm not a morning person. I'll probably see you at school later on.'

'I hope so. Goodnight, Kate.' He shook her hand very formally. 'Thank you for your company.'

Once she reached her room Kate rang reception to order breakfast there instead of in the dining room as she would have much preferred. Having dinner with a stranger was one thing, breakfast a different thing entirely. Philip Brace, she suspected, was another man finding it hard to adjust to single status.

Kate's phone rang when she was settled down in bed with a book. She checked the caller ID and smiled smugly. 'Hello, Jack.'

'Are you in your room?' he asked, 'or have I interrupted your dinner?'

'I've had dinner. I'm reading in bed.'

'Anna Maitland told me where you were this weekend. Why couldn't you have told me?'

'Last time we spoke you weren't exactly friendly.'

'I'd just heard you'd been to the theatre with Forster.'

'It's not against the law.'

'True. Why didn't you tell me where you were going this weekend?'

'To be honest, Jack, it never occurred to me.'

'God, you're a cruel woman!'

'Why did you want to speak to me tonight?'

'Must I have a reason?'

'It's a bit late for a chat,' she said tartly.

'I waited until now to avoid interrupting your dinner. Was it good?'

'Very good indeed.'

'Did you dine alone?'

Kate ground her teeth. 'As it happens, no. The father of one of the other pupils is staying here. He suggested we join forces.'

'Is he with you now?'

'No, Jack,' she snapped. 'I told you. I'm in bed.'

Jack chuckled. 'You're annoyed.'

'Such intuition! Is that why you rang? To annoy me?'

'No. I rang to invite you to dinner at Mill House next Saturday. With the Maitlands and the Beresfords.'

'Ah. Lucy won't be livid after all, then.'

'Run that past me again?'

'I spoke to Anna earlier. She didn't know you'd invited Mrs Beresford.'

'Were you offended because I hadn't asked you?'

'Not in the least. You're obviously repaying Anna's hospitality. You haven't had any from me.'

'No,' he agreed with a sigh, 'just hostility.'

'Nonsense. I've given you coffee.'

'Did you give Richard Forster coffee?'

'No. He left me very correctly on my doorstep.'

'Are you seeing him again?'

Kate bristled. 'As a matter of fact, he suggested dinner tonight, but Jo had a prior call on my time.'

'Good. If he suggests next Saturday, tell him *I* have a prior call on your time.'

'I most certainly will not. Besides, I haven't accepted your invitation yet, Jack.'

'You mean you've got some other man on a string as well?'

'I could be seeing Philip Brace.'

'Who the hell is he?'

'The man I had dinner with tonight. He lives in Worcester. It's not far to drive.'

'Do you intend seeing him again?'

'None of your business, Jack.'

Instead of hanging up on her as Kate half expected Jack laughed in her ear. 'It is, you know. Are you coming next Saturday or not?'

'I might as well.'

'I'll take that as a yes.' He paused. 'By the way, are you having breakfast with your new friend in the morning?'

'Yes,' lied Kate angrily, and disconnected, seething. Jack had absolutely no right to interfere in her social life. If she wanted to see other men she would, damn his eyes. But as she calmed down she was forced to admit the unpalatable truth. Compared with Jack Logan, all other men paled into insignificance.

Kate would have felt a whole lot better if she could have seen Jack pacing round his kitchen at Mill House at that very moment, cursing himself for behaving like a jealous schoolboy. He was supposed to be patient, he reminded himself savagely. The plan was to win her back, not drive her away for good. He stopped dead so suddenly he stepped on Bran, who yelped in anguish. As he stroked the dog in apology Jack gave thanks for the second chance life had given him. This time he would make sure he took full advantage of it. He'd had no thought of marrying again, ever, until he'd met up with Kate again. He'd made work his life. But work was no longer enough. He wanted Kate back in his life for good this time, as his wife. When the time was right he'd tell her that and put his mother's ring back on her finger where it belonged.

There was no sign of Philip Brace when Kate arrived at the school next day and she drove Joanna back to lunch at the hotel with a light heart, prepared to savour every minute as her companion chattered happily throughout the deliberately careful journey.

The meal was a conventional roast, and Joanna ate hugely and then wandered with Kate in the hotel grounds in the pale winter sunshine afterwards.

'I've got another Sunday out before the end of term,' she informed Kate. 'But no Saturday.'

'Never mind. I'll drive over and back the same day, but you can still eat here if you like.'

'Is it very expensive?' asked Jo anxiously.

'No,' said Kate firmly. 'It's starting to rain. Let's watch television before tea.'

'I get tea as well?' said Jo rapturously.

'You bet.' Kate cast an eye at the slender, long-legged child, already as tall as her aunt. 'Where do you put it all?'

The afternoon passed far too quickly for Kate, but to her relief they arrived at the school just after Emma and Jane, Jo's bosom pals. In the flurry of introductions to parents and the comparisons the girls were making about their lunch, the dreaded parting was less painful than expected and Kate was halfway home before she remembered Philip Brace.

It was an unpleasant journey, with sleet slithering against the windscreen all the way. Her brightly lit house was a hugely welcome sight when Kate eventually turned into Park Crescent, and with a sigh of relief she locked the car, hurried into the house, deactivated the alarm, then locked her front door and threw the bolts. She'd turned off her mobile phone rather than have it ring while she was driving, and as half-expected there was a message waiting from Jack demanding a call when she got home.

She reported in to Anna first and then rang Jack.

'I'm back,' she said, in response to the barked 'Logan' in her ear.

'Thank God for that; I was worried. It's a hell of a night.'

'Tell me about it. Freezing fog added to driving sleet for the last few miles.'

'Do you have the right kind of phone in your car?'

'No.'

'Then get one, Kate. It's only common sense when you're driving long distances alone.'

'Yes, Dad.'

'I'm not your father!'

'True. You're my friend.'

He breathed in audibly. 'How was your day? Did your niece have a good time?'

'I think so. She certainly ate well. Jo must have a fantastic metabolism; she's as slender as a reed.'

'Takes after her aunt. By the way, did you manage to avoid your dinner partner today?'

'I forgot all about him when I took Jo back to school. I was too busy being bright and cheerful to give him a thought.'

'Good.'

'Why good, Jack?'

'Save your thoughts for me, Kate. I'll be in touch before Saturday. Sleep well.'

Kate woke next morning to the discovery that she'd slept very well indeed. During the week she had spent restless nights, worrying over what she would find when she saw Jo again. But reassurance over Joanna had combined with a tiring journey home and the gratifying chat with Jack to give Kate her best night's sleep for quite a while.

When the Suttons decided to send Joanna away to school Kate had been against the idea, convinced that the child would be miserable away from her family at the tender age of eight. But Jo had taken to boarding school life like a duck to water. And when Elizabeth and Robert were so cruelly removed from her young life the security of the familiar school background was a contributing factor in helping Jo to cope with her loss. And she still has me, thought Kate, as she wrote to Jo to tell her how much she'd enjoyed their weekend together. She made no mention of the extra care she'd taken on the drive back to ensure the safety of one of the few relatives Joanna Sutton had left in the world.

CHAPTER SIX

THE prospect of dinner at Mill House added a tinge of excitement to a week that was busier than usual. After Kate's weekend away she was obliged to labour hard and long to finish the dining room in the time left over from the work that brought in the money. She even refused an invitation to supper with Anna and Ben mid week, too tired by evening for anything more strenuous than a bath and an early night.

'I'll be seeing you on Saturday, anyway,' she said, when Anna objected.

'I was hoping you'd come shopping with me on Friday first, Kate. I need something new for Saturday.'

'You've got loads of clothes.'

'I can't get into the formal stuff. My waistline's expanding by the day. Lord knows what I'll be like by the time Junior actually arrives.'

In the end Kate agreed to an hour's shopping before the afternoon painting session. 'But one hour only,' she warned.

The hour expanded into an entire afternoon with a tea break incorporated into it, rather than afterwards in Park Crescent, due to Anna's aversion to paint smells.

'Can't cope in my condition,' said Anna, eyeing her reflection in a changing room. 'What do you think? The silk tunic and skirt, or the dress I tried on first.'

'That shade of blue looks great on you,' said Kate, and grinned. 'But so does the black dress. Buy both. Ben won't mind.'

Anna took the advice she wanted to hear, but no amount of coaxing persuaded Kate to buy something.

'I've got enough from my former life to last me for ages.

No point in wasting money on something new.' Kate patted Anna's hand. 'I promise I won't let you down again. No jeans this time.'

'You didn't let me down,' protested her friend. 'You made all the other women green with envy. Did you wear jeans when you had dinner with Jack?'

Kate shook her head. 'I thought we were eating out, so I honoured him with the dress intended for your party—the one I wore at your place at Christmas.'

'The drop-dead job with the cleavage?' Anna grinned. 'That must have got his juices flowing.'

'Is pregnancy to blame for this sudden earthiness of yours, Mrs Maitland?'

'No, just for my appetite. I need tea and cream cakes right now!'

By the time Anna dropped her off at home Kate had lost all enthusiasm for more painting. There was only one wall left to do and that, she decided, could wait. Now she had a sitting room worthy of the name she would spoil herself and stretch out on her new chaise to read instead of doing any one of a long list of things she should be doing instead. She enjoyed a whole hour deep in the intricacies of a courtroom thriller before the telephone rang to spoil her fun.

'Richard here, Kate. How are you?'

'I'm well. How are things with you?'

'Busy. Did you enjoy your weekend?'

'I did, very much. Nasty journey back, but it was worth it.'

'I'm sure it was. Look, Kate, I know this is short notice, but are you free tomorrow? A film, meal, anything you like.'

'Sorry, Richard. I'm already booked for dinner tomorrow.'

Kate could feel her face growing pink during a pause which lasted too long for comfort.

'Is that the truth?' he asked at last, 'or is it your way of letting me down lightly?'

'Richard,' said Kate on impulse. 'Are you going home about now?'

'Yes. I'm just locking up.'

'Would you like to call here for a drink first?'

'Of course I would. See you soon.'

Kate checked on the contents of the fridge and went back to the sitting room to her book. When she heard a car stop outside she put a marker in her page and got up to answer the door, then stared in dismay.

'You were expecting someone else?' Jack inquired sardonically.

'Yes, I am.' She shrugged. 'It's a bit awkward, but come in, if you like.'

'But you'd rather I made myself scarce.'

'Yes, please. I'll explain later.'

He threw her a flinty look, strode to the Jensen at the kerb and drove off with a growl of engine just as Richard Forster's car turned into the Crescent.

'Was that Logan?' he asked as he got out.

'Yes. Do come in.'

Kate showed him into the sitting room. 'I can offer you beer or a glass of wine. Or medicinal brandy,' she added as an afterthought, feeling rather in need of one herself.

'Beer would be good. Attractive house,' he added, looking round.

'Thank you. I won't be a moment.' Kate took a can of beer and a tonic from the fridge, filled two glasses and went back to the sitting room.

Richard took the beer and stood in front of the fireplace with the air of a man not expecting to stay long. 'You've asked me here for a reason, Kate,' he said without preamble. 'Will you tell me what it is?'

'It seemed better to talk to you face to face.' She drank some of her tonic. 'Firstly, I really am going out on Saturday night.' At least she hoped so.

'Firstly means a secondly coming up,' he said dryly.

She nodded. 'I have a question to ask. You don't have to answer it, of course.'

He looked at her with steady blue eyes. 'Ask away.'

'Are you still in love with your wife?'

Richard blinked, startled, as though this was the last thing he'd expected. He was silent for a long time, his face like a mask, then shrugged, his eyes hard. 'Yes,' he said bitterly. 'I am.'

Kate nodded. 'I thought so.'

'Because you're still in love with Logan?' he said, startling her in turn.

'I used to be, once,' she admitted.

'Is he taking you out on Saturday?'

'Not exactly. He's asked me to a dinner party at his house—with other guests,' she added.

Richard drank some of his beer, eyeing her over the rim of his glass. 'I've heard that entertaining at home isn't the Logan style.'

'So have I.'

Richard put the glass down on the table, and looked Kate in the eye. 'It's now established that you have a prior engagement on Saturday, but why, exactly, did you ask about my wife?'

'Look, Richard,' said Kate, taking the bull by the horns, 'I don't think casual dating is your kind of thing. If I've got a colossal nerve to think you'd want something less casual with me, I apologise, humbly. But I thought it best to say, face to face—'

'That a relationship of any kind between us is out of the question?'

'Yes, Richard. And not because I don't like you, because I do, very much. But my gut feeling tells me that the only relationship you really want is with your wife.'

For a moment Kate thought he would make a furious denial, but after a fraught silence Richard nodded grimly. 'Your instinct is right. I do want her back, for all the good it will do me.'

'Is she involved with someone else?'

'Not as far as I know. Caroline's a journalist and her sole passion is her job.'

'She might be finding it isn't enough by now. Have you asked her?'

'No.' His eyes hardened again. 'I refuse to go crawling. It's up to her to make the first move.'

Kate shook her head impatiently. 'Oh, come on! Forget all that macho nonsense. If you want her, make the first move yourself.'

Richard's jaw clenched, and for a moment Kate was afraid he was going to tell her to shut up and mind her own business. But eventually a wry smile dawned in his eyes and she breathed a sigh of relief. 'Maybe you're right, Kate,' he said at last. 'I'll go down to the flat on Sunday.'

'Why leave it until then? Go tomorrow.'

'She works on Saturdays.' His mouth twisted. 'The sky would fall in if Caroline knocked off before her beloved newspaper's ready for Sunday breakfast tables.'

'Insist that she does.'

'Carry her out over my shoulder?' he said, laughing, suddenly a different man from the wary lawyer of minutes earlier.

'Why not?'

'Why not, indeed!' Richard drained his glass and got up. 'OK, I'll give it a whirl. Have you ever considered a career in Relate?' he added.

She grimaced. 'Absolutely not. This is my first—and last—venture into marriage counselling!'

He shook her hand formally as she saw him to the door. 'Shall I let you know what happens?'

'Yes, please. Good luck!'

Kate waved him off, then rang Jack.

'What the blazes was all that about?' he demanded.

'Where are you?'

'I'm with Dad.'

'Can you come round for a minute?'

'You just threw me out.'

'If you want to know why, come back. Or not,' she added crossly. 'Up to you, Jack.'

'It had better be good,' he said ominously.

This time when Kate threw open the door Jack just stood there, waiting, tall and formidable and very much the head of Logan Development in a dark suit and long dark overcoat. 'Don't just stand there,' she said irritably. 'Come in.'

'If you're quite sure I'm not interrupting something,' he said with sarcasm.

'Oh, don't be difficult, Jack. Do you want a drink?' Kate turned her back on him and went along the hall to the kitchen.

Jack closed the door behind him and followed her. 'Have you got a beer?'

'Yes.' She handed him a can and fetched a glass. 'I've also got half a tonic waiting in the sitting room, so let's go in there.'

'You mean I'd better be sitting comfortably when you tell me what's up? I saw Forster arrive as I took off just now,' he added.

Kate threw him an exasperated look as they went back to the other room. She drew the curtains and switched on lamps and resumed her chair. Jack slung his coat on the end of the chaise and leaned back against the curved support, looking far more at ease than her previous visitor.

'Richard asked me out on Saturday night, Jack.'

'No surprise there.' He shot her a look. 'I hope you told him you were otherwise engaged.'

'Of course I did,' she said impatiently, and drank some tonic. 'But I suggested he came round on his way home so I could talk to him face to face.'

Jack leaned forward, his eyes suddenly intent. 'Why?'

'Richard had to be told that a relationship with me was never going to happen.'

The eyes narrowed. 'Anything to do with me?'

She shook her head. 'No, Jack, nothing at all. There's just no place in my life for any relationship of that kind right now, with you, Richard or anyone else. But that's irrelevant anyway, because he's still in love with his wife.'

Jack sat back, eyebrows raised, and drank some of his beer. 'Did he admit that?'

'Eventually, yes. At first he went all tight-lipped and said it was up to her to make the first move. But in the end he changed his mind and he's off to London tomorrow to make the move himself.'

'Because you told him to?'

'Because I advised him,' she corrected. 'He's a lawyer, remember.'

Jack raised an eyebrow. 'What happens if she shuts the door in his face? Will he come rushing back to cry on your shoulder?'

'If he does, all he'll get is sympathy. The situation remains unchanged.'

'The situation being?'

'That Joanna takes precedence over everything else in my life right now.'

Jack's mood changed abruptly. 'Of course. How is she, Kate? You said she enjoyed her time with you last weekend.'

'She seems to be coping remarkably well.'

He eyed her searchingly. 'But what happens at night, after lights out in her dormitory?'

Touched by his insight, Kate repeated the account given by Dr Knight. 'Jo's dealing with her loss far better than I ever imagined.'

'Having you as a guardian is a lot to do with it.'

'It's kind of you to say so, Jack.'

He grinned suddenly. 'Don't sound so surprised. I can be very kind when I put my mind to it.'

'I know that. So did Dawn Taylor.' Kate could have kicked herself when she saw Jack's smile vanish.

He abandoned his beer and got up. 'Time I was on my way. Thanks for the drink.'

Kate jumped up and put a hand on his arm. 'Do you have plans for this evening, Jack?'

He looked down at the hand. 'Why?'

'If you haven't, you could stay to supper. If you like,' she muttered, already regretting her impulse.

Jack's grin was back as he looked up. 'Thought you'd never ask.'

'You'll have to eat whatever I can find in the cupboard,' she warned, surprised to feel so relieved. 'Come into the kitchen while I forage.'

'I've got a better idea,' he said, sitting down again. 'Let's order in. You can impress me with your culinary skill next time.'

Kate returned to her chair, smiling gratefully. 'I won't say no. I've had a tiring afternoon.'

'Painting?'

'No, far more exhausting than that. I went on a shopping trip with Anna. She needed something to wear to your dinner party. Her current wardrobe doesn't fit.' Kate swirled the remains of her drink round her glass. 'Just between you and me, she's pregnant, and jubilant about it. So is Ben.'

'I can imagine he would be! Should I congratulate them?'

'I'm not sure if they've gone public on it, so maybe not yet.'

'My lips shall remain sealed. Would you have another beer?'

Kate went to fetch more drinks, and found Jack talking on his phone when she got back.

He closed it with a snap. 'That was Dad, worried something

was wrong. So I told him you'd asked me to supper and right now he's probably jumping joyfully to all the wrong conclusions.'

Kate handed him a beer, topped up her own glass and sat down. 'It's just supper, Jack.'

The black-lashed eyes gleamed as he pulled the tab on the can. 'But Dad will take it as a sign that you're thawing towards me. Are you?' he added.

'Yes.' Kate smiled at him cheerfully. 'I knew I'd upset you and wanted to show I was sorry.'

'In that case, let's see if we can manage the rest of the evening without coming to blows.' He gave her a sharp look. 'Not that I would ever, in any circumstances, raise a hand to you, Kate.'

'I know that,' she said impatiently. 'You can't have changed that much.'

His eyes held hers. 'I haven't changed at all when it comes to the important things in life.'

'Neither have I.' She grinned. 'As usual, I fancy some Chinese.'

He rolled his eyes. 'Let me guess—same old sweet and sour pork, spare ribs and spring rolls.'

'You remember!' She nodded with enthusiasm. 'With crispy seaweed on the side and masses of fried rice. I've got a menu in the kitchen. Shall I order now? I'm hungry.'

They sat at the kitchen table later, facing each other across a sea of foil dishes. Jack had discarded his jacket and rolled up his shirtsleeves when Kate provided large tea towels in lieu of napkins.

'Can't get grease on your bespoke suiting,' she said briskly.

'Amen to that. Next time I wear jeans. Because,' Jack added deliberately, 'there will be a next time, Kate.'

She shrugged. 'Why not? No harm in a takeaway now and then.'

They shunted dishes back and forth, emptying them with

hunger as Jack told her he'd called in to make sure she hadn't backed out of the dinner party. Assured that she was looking forward to it with bated breath, he grinned and began to talk about his latest restoration venture. Kate listened with keen interest as he described the transformation of a disused factory into affordable flats.

'No pricey loft apartments like the one you shared with fiancé mark two,' he told her, and nodded wryly at her startled look. 'Oh yes, news filtered through to me eventually. Unlike your banker a lot of people can't afford that kind of thing, but they still want comfort and style. This project will provide both. The building's user-friendly, and will include smaller apartments for first time buyers and a children's nursery school.'

'Convenient for shopping and schools for older children?' Kate asked, breaking open a fortune cookie.

'Only ten minutes from both. The wasteland around it will be landscaped into gardens to provide as green an environment as possible.'

'It sounds wonderful, Jack.'

'When it's nearer completion I'll take you over it.' He leaned over to read her fortune. 'New horizons are opening for you,' he intoned solemnly.

'Pretty general sort of forecast,' said Kate, and handed him a cookie.

Jack broke it open. 'You are about to receive your heart's desire!' he read.

'You're kidding!'

'Alas, yes,' he said, grinning. 'Mine's the same as yours.'

Kate bundled the debris into a waste sack and ran hot water and detergent into the kitchen sink. 'You go up to the bathroom and wash—last door on the landing at the back,' she told Jack. 'I'll scrub my grease off down here.'

He returned a few minutes later. 'I resisted the temptation to explore,' he said self-righteously.

'You can take a look if you like.'

'I'd rather you showed me round.'

Kate felt like a proud parent showing off its child as she led the way upstairs.

'This is where I work,' she said, at the threshold of her study. 'Jo is next door, in the blue and yellow room. And I'm through here.' She led him across the landing to her newly painted bedroom, then opened the door on the bathroom with the tub Ben had found for her in a reclamation yard. 'That's the lot. If you were a prospective buyer, how would it strike you?'

'Any smart young couple would go mad for it,' Jack assured her. 'But you don't intend to sell, surely?'

'No. I just wanted an objective opinion. I've never done any decorating before.' She pulled a face. 'The preparation is the hardest part. Once I get to the actual painting, it's easy.' She held out her hands ruefully. 'They'll never be the same again.'

'Wear gloves!'

'I do, most of the time. But you can't wear them for everything.'

'True,' said Jack, and turned to look at the mahogany sleigh bed visible through the open doorway to Kate's room. 'I assume that belonged to the famous Aunt Edith?'

She nodded. 'Impressive, isn't it! They make good copies these days, but this is the real McCoy. The auctioneer who came here to value the other furniture salivated when he saw it and offered me a good price, but I refused to part with it.'

'Very wise. If he was salivating, the price was probably half of what it should have been.'

'Cynic!'

'Realist,' he contradicted, and took her hands in his. 'Shall I kiss them better?'

Kate stood very still, suddenly aware that the door to her

bedroom stood open in invitation. She looked up into Jack's eyes and felt her knees tremble.

'Shall I?' he repeated, his voice deepening.

Kate watched mutely as he lifted each hand to his lips in turn, the touch of his open mouth on her skin sending her pulse into overdrive. 'Thank you,' she said hoarsely. 'Much better—'

The rest of her words were smothered against his mouth as Jack pulled her into his arms and kissed her hungrily, his lips and tongue so irresistible she melted against him, her heart pounding as his hands slid beneath her sweater. She felt a familiar, liquid rush of hot response as his kiss deepened and, without taking his lips from hers, Jack picked her up and carried her through the door of her room. But when he laid her down on the bed Kate rolled to the far side and stood up, shaking her head in vehement rejection.

Jack stood breathing heavily, his eyes hard as flint. 'Why not?' he demanded harshly.

Kate brushed past him out of the room and hurried down the steep staircase, her knees trembling. It was her fault. Jack Logan was a man, after all, and a man who had once been her lover. She didn't blame him for wanting to make love to her, but she couldn't let that happen. She wasn't laying herself open to that kind of pain again.

Jack came into the kitchen behind her and picked up his jacket. 'Kate,' he said harshly, 'all you had to do was say no.'

She turned on him, eyes flashing. 'I know that.'

He raked a hand through his hair, his eyes angry. 'Then why in God's name make me feel like a rapist?'

She let out a deep, unsteady sigh. 'I told you that friendship with me would be hard work, Jack.'

'So you did.'

Kate eyed him uncertainly as he shrugged into his jacket. 'If you'd rather I didn't turn up tomorrow, I quite understand.'

He stared at her in disbelief. 'And what reason will you give your friends for staying away?'

She bit her lip. 'Migraine, stomach bug, whatever.'

'And when Anna Maitland comes rushing here to check up on you?'

'I don't let her in because she's pregnant and I might be contagious.'

Jack slid into his overcoat, looking at her steadily. 'Kate, I vote we delete the past few minutes and go back to the supper we shared. I enjoyed the evening up to that point and, unless you were putting on an act, you did too.'

'Of course I did.'

'So stop behaving like an idiot and come to Mill House tomorrow as you promised.' Jack's lips twitched. 'You know you want to see Lucy Beresford's reaction to the house.'

Kate laughed unwillingly. 'True. All right, Jack,' she said, resigned, and looked at him squarely. 'I apologise.'

'For what, exactly?'

'For being late with my no. It won't happen again.'

'Next time you'll say yes?'

'There's never going to be a yes, Jack,' she said with such emphasis his eyes narrowed.

They stared into hers for a long, tense interval, then he shrugged. 'Never say never, Kate.' He smiled suddenly.

'What now?'

'Did your aunt sleep alone in that erotic bed?'

'As far as I know, she did.' Kate grinned. 'Though, somehow, I never thought of her as my *maiden* aunt.'

'You think she had lovers?'

'She was in the army in the Second World War, so she probably had more than one. And she worked in London as some tycoon's right hand for years afterwards. She bought this house with money he left her in his will, so maybe their relationship was closer than she let on. Apparently my father was surprised that she chose to come back here to live.'

'Obviously a family trait,' said Jack dryly, and took Kate's hand with the care of someone handling a stick of gelignite. 'Are we on track again? If friendship's the only thing on offer, I'll settle for it. But I won't lie to you, Kate. I want more than that.'

'That's all there is, Jack,' she said flatly.

'The chemistry's still there,' he pointed out, and released her hand. 'You felt it just as much as I did before something put on the brakes. So I repeat. Never say never.'

CHAPTER SEVEN

KATE had fully intended taking Saturday off to get in the mood for Jack's dinner party. Instead she went on with her painting with the radio turned up high, trying to drag her mind away from the few brief, heated moments that had given her such a frustrated, restless night. She was the guilty one—or the stupid one. It was herself she'd been fighting, not Jack. For one desperate moment she'd wanted to pull him down on the bed and make love with him until the world went away.

Her face set in determined lines as she put her painting paraphernalia away later. The solution was simple. If she was never alone with Jack again it couldn't happen. But that would mean no more impromptu suppers. Her shoulders sagged. It had been so good to spend time with him again and just talk. Quite apart from the unique physical chemistry between them, Jack had once been the best friend she'd ever had. She'd been madly in love with him, but she'd also liked him better than any man she'd met before or since. The loss of friend as well as lover had made the pain and disillusion even harder to bear when it all ended in tears.

The doorbell rang just as Kate was about to go upstairs for a bath. She opened the door to find a young woman proffering a flower arrangement.

'Kate Durant?' she asked. 'These are for you.'

'Thank you,' said Kate, surprised, and hurried inside to read the card attached to the basket.

'For Katie,' said the message.

Kate blinked hard as she looked at the delicate blend of freesias and miniature tulips. She set the basket of flowers on the table in the sitting room and stood back to admire, her new resolution wavering already. The subtle colours blended so perfectly with the room—Jack had obviously chosen them personally. Afraid to trust her voice she thanked him via a text message.

'We were going to offer to come and pick you up tonight,' Anna rang later to inform her. 'But it occurred to me that you'd rather drive yourself. You might—' cough '—want to stay on for a bit after we've gone home.'

'I very much doubt that, but there's no point in coming miles out of your way to collect me,' said Kate tartly. 'I'll drive myself.'

'You sound a bit snappy!'

'Sorry, sorry. I've just finished the last wall in the dining room and I'm a bit tired.'

'For heaven's sake, Kate,' said Anna in exasperation, 'surely you could have taken the day off today of all days! No wonder you sound on edge.'

'Why should I be on edge?'

'I assume that it's dinner for six tonight?'

'I think so.'

'Then Lucy Beresford—the biggest gossip in town—will take it for granted that you and Jack are, or are intending to be, a couple too.'

'Oh, God! I hadn't thought of that.'

'Well, I had. Have you seen Jack lately?'

'We shared a Chinese here last night.'

'Does this mean you're getting back with him, then?' Anna demanded.

'No. At least not in the way you mean.'

'Pity. Now tell me what you're wearing so we don't clash.'

Kate had signed on with a doctor, and even with Anna's dentist, but had never made it to a hairdresser. She wished she had, later, when her hair refused to behave. Her intention had been a sleek, sophisticated knot to wear with her sleek, sophisticated suit, but her slippery hair refused to stay up, and after a while she gave in and left it loose. But when she viewed the overall effect with the suit she wasn't unhappy. No cleavage or anything clinging tonight, not even jewellery, other than her gold watch. The mannish tailoring of her black velvet trousers and jacket was softened only by the gleam of a white silk camisole. And, because the weather was no more in party mood than she was, Kate pulled knee-length black boots over the velvet trousers to protect them from the pouring rain, belted on her trench coat, switched on the burglar alarm, locked the door behind her and stood under the shelter of the door pediment to aim the remote at her little two-seater.

When Kate reached Mill House the door was standing open and Jack, wearing a more casual suit than usual, came to meet her with a golf umbrella.

'Hi,' she said brightly. 'What a night! Am I the first?'

'Yes. Come and talk to Bran before I banish him to the boot room.'

'Hold on, I'm just collecting my shoes.'

When she slid from the car Jack shouted, 'Sit,' to the retriever as he came bounding towards her in welcome, and Kate bent to scratch Bran's ear, full of admiration when he obeyed his master instead of jumping all over her as he obviously wanted to.

'You are so gorgeous,' she told him, and Jack laughed.

'Just like his master.'

'You wish!'

The dog trotted happily beside them as they went inside. In the small outer hall Kate exchanged her boots for the silver-heeled black silk shoes and handed her coat to Jack, her eyebrows raised when he stood looking at her in silence.

'You don't approve?' she demanded. 'Should I have worn a dress?'

'You look sensational and you know it,' he said gruffly. 'Your hair looks hellish sexy like that with the tailored suit.'

'I wasn't aiming for sexy,' she protested.

'Then God help me when you do!'

'Did you get my message about the flowers, Jack?' she said hastily. 'They were lovely. Thank you.'

'I aim to please.' He clicked his fingers to the dog. 'I'll hang your coat in the boot room. Come and meet Molly.'

Two women turned round from the range, smiling, as Jack led Kate into the kitchen.

'Ladies, this is my friend, Kate Durant,' he announced.

'I'm Molly Carter,' said the young one, surprising Kate. 'This is my mum, Hazel. She's helping out tonight.'

'Nice to meet you,' said Hazel, a neat figure in a white lawn apron over a black dress. 'I'm just the help. Molly does the cooking.'

'And it's wonderful,' Kate assured her. 'I tasted some of it the other night!'

Molly smiled, pleased. Small and sturdy in jeans and vast white apron, with blonde hair in a braid down her back, she was much younger than Kate had expected. 'I hope you like the menu for tonight. It's simple because the boss thought it best not to be too adventurous, but I hope it will suit everybody.'

'No doubt about that,' Kate assured her, as Jack came back from exiling Bran.

'Right then, Kate,' he said briskly. 'Let's have a drink before the others arrive. Any bits and pieces, Molly?'

'Cold ones on the coffee table, Boss, hot ones to follow when the others arrive,' she informed him, and went back to stirring something in a saucepan.

Kate followed Jack to the main room and stopped in her tracks. Spring flowers in a shallow creamware bowl sat between the promised dishes of canapés on the big rosewood table, but the sight that brought a smile to her face was the pile of large suede cushions stacked either end of the sofa.

Jack's lips twitched. 'Forster isn't the only one who can

take advice,' he said smugly. 'You mentioned something about cushions and a flower arrangement, I believe?'

She gave a snort of laughter. 'I wasn't *serious*, Jack!'

'Now she tells me. What do you think? The official colours, I was informed, are caramel and mocha.'

'You bought them here in town?'

He nodded as he removed the cork from a bottle of champagne. 'And I ordered the flowers the same time as yours, but Molly did the arranging.'

'Your Molly's quite a star, isn't she? But she looks so young!'

'After catering college she couldn't find a job which paid enough, so she answered my advertisement. She's saving to open a place of her own one day.' Jack filled two glasses and handed one to Kate.

'Then I hope you pay her well!'

'I do. And will pay more like a shot if someone tries to steal her from me.' He touched his glass to hers. 'Let's drink a toast to my first dinner party.'

'I've eaten dinner here before,' she reminded him.

'That was just family supper with Dad. Tonight's entertainment is more ambitious—a first at Mill House.'

'Why now?'

Jack shrugged. 'I decided it was time to repay hospitality at home.'

'You may regret it,' Kate said ruefully. 'After tonight, according to Anna, Lucy Beresford will be convinced we're a couple.'

'Don't worry,' he said casually. 'At the Maitland party I told her that we'd known each other in the past. As far as she's concerned, I've merely invited an old friend to make up the numbers.'

'Thanks a lot!' Kate chuckled. 'More flattery like that and I'll get above myself.'

PLAY THE
Lucky Key Game

and you can get

Do You Have the LUCKY KEY?

FREE BOOKS
and # FREE GIFTS!

Scratch the gold areas with a coin. Then check below to see the books and gifts you can get!

YES!
I have scratched off the gold areas. Please send me the **2 FREE BOOKS** and **2 FREE GIFTS** for which I qualify. I understand I am under no obligation to purchase any books, as explained on the back of this card.

306 HDL EF5D   106 HDL EF53

FIRST NAME   LAST NAME

ADDRESS

APT.#   CITY

STATE/PROV.   ZIP/POSTAL CODE

www.eHarlequin.com

2 free books plus 2 free gifts   1 free book

2 free books   Try Again!

Offer limited to one per household and not valid to current Harlequin Presents® subscribers.
Your Privacy – Harlequin is committed to protecting your privacy. Our Privacy Policy is available online at www.eHarlequin.com or upon request from the Harlequin Reader Service. From time to time we make our lists of customers available to reputable firms who may have a product or service of interest to you. If you would prefer for us not to share your name and address, please check here. ☐

DETACH AND MAIL CARD TODAY!

(H-P-04/07)

© 2002 HARLEQUIN ENTERPRISES LTD. ® and ™ are trademarks owned and used by the trademark owner and/or its licensee.

Jack grinned and offered her the canapés. 'Lucy needn't know your support was vital to calm my nerves.'

'Nerves, my foot!' Kate bit into a delicious combination of shrimp and meltingly light pastry. 'Yum, these are delicious! Molly made them herself, of course?'

'As you say, she's a star—and, don't worry, I'm paying her a bonus; Hazel, too.' Jack looked at his watch. 'The others should be here any minute.'

'Let's wander into the hall, then. My sole reason for being here is to see the reaction when your guests arrive.'

'Is that true, Kate?'

She sipped some of her drink and threw a smile at him over her shoulder as she strolled across the hall to the fireplace to look up at the portrait. 'No, of course not.'

He followed her and stood so close she felt his breath on her neck. 'Am I forgiven for last night, Katie?'

'No forgiveness necessary or required, Jack.' She turned to smile at him as tyres crunched wetly outside. 'Show time.'

A peal on the doorbell brought muffled barking from Bran in the boot room as Jack went to admit his remaining guests, Hazel following to collect umbrellas and raincoats. 'Good evening, everyone,' Kate heard him say. 'Welcome to Mill House.'

The Beresfords came in first, George balding and fifty-something with twinkling eyes, his wife forty going on eighteen in a pink prom dress. Lucy's eyes widened as she took in her surroundings, then narrowed in swift speculation when she saw Kate standing near the fireplace.

'How nice to see you again,' she said, rushing to join her. 'Isn't this the most marvellous house? What a romantic driveway, Jack.'

Kate said the appropriate things and turned to kiss Anna. 'You look ravishing in your new blue, Mrs Maitland.'

'Thanks, friend. Clever of you to wear black with this background,' Anna murmured. 'What a place!'

Ben came to kiss Kate and Jack ushered them all into the main room, avoiding Kate's eyes as Lucy went into more high-decibel raptures. Jack provided champagne; Hazel came in with a platter of hot canapés and Kate stood with George near the fireplace, answering questions about the house she'd inherited.

'I've been dying to see *your* house.' Anna smiled demurely at Jack. 'Kate's told me so much about it.'

Lucy glanced across at Kate, sharp-eyed. 'You've been here before?'

'My father knew Kate when she lived here in the town as a child,' said Jack blandly. 'He insisted I invited her to kitchen supper to talk about old times.'

Anna choked on a mouthful of pastry and Ben proffered a napkin.

'Steady the buffs,' he murmured, smiling at Kate.

Conversation grew general with the second glass of champagne, and by the time Hazel returned to announce dinner Jack Logan's first guests at Mill House were in mellow mood.

The dining room was smaller and more intimate than the main room, but Jack had kept to his white theme for the walls, with a large pencil drawing of Bran as the only artwork. The furniture was modern and very plain, the table set with white porcelain and gleaming crystal, which reflected flames from thick white candles in heavy glass holders. Once everyone was seated, Hazel came in to offer a choice of lobster ravioli or pears with Stilton for the first course.

'Molly thought the lobster might not suit everyone,' said Jack, smiling. 'Being a mere male such things never occurred to me.'

'You need a woman in your life, Jack,' said Lucy, and gazed at her husband in wide-eyed innocence when he frowned at her.

'Anna says you've finished your decorating, Kate,' said Ben swiftly.

'I certainly have.' She smiled at him. 'My garden's the next thing on the agenda.'

'You're so self-sufficient!' exclaimed Lucy. 'Anna tells me you've painted your entire house yourself. Amazing. I wouldn't know where to start. Did you go on a course?'

'No, I just cheated a bit. I had the ceilings, cornices and gloss paint done by a professional before I moved from London. He relined the walls too, ready for me to start painting. I finished the last room this very afternoon,' said Kate.

Anna smiled at her affectionately. 'Thank goodness for that. I hate the smell of paint.'

'No wonder, in your condition—' Lucy bit her lip, eyeing Ben in contrition. 'Sorry. My big mouth.'

'Not to worry,' said Ben easily, and smiled across the table at his wife. 'This is as good a time as any to make the announcement. We're expecting our first child in the autumn.'

Jack sprang up to shake Ben by the hand, careful to avoid Kate's eyes as he asked permission to kiss the mother-to-be. 'Congratulations. Let me give you some more champagne.'

Anna shook her head regretfully. 'I've had my quota for tonight. Mineral water from now on, please.'

It was a very animated gathering who went on to eat hot glazed ham with spinach soufflé, followed by simple, perfect apple pie and local cheese served with Molly's savoury biscuits. When they went back to the main room the fire had been replenished and a dish of *petit fours* placed beside a coffee tray.

'Marvellous meal,' said Anna, sitting by Kate with a sigh. 'My compliments to the chef, Jack.'

'I'll pass them on to her.' He smiled at Kate. 'If you'll pour the coffee, I'll pass the cups round. Hazel's helping Molly clear up.'

Having diligently avoided the slightest suggestion of acting as hostess up to that point, Kate had to give in about the coffee, conscious of Lucy Beresford's eyes boring into her as she filled the cups. Jack could do what he liked with the cakes, she decided, and leaned against a suede cushion beside Anna, out of range of Lucy's eagle eye. But Lucy wasn't done with her.

'I hear you have the most extraordinary job, Kate,' she said, leaning forward in her chair. 'Anna says you work from home as a virtual assistant. What on earth does that mean?'

Kate gave a brief, succinct explanation.

'She works with five clients, and doesn't make coffee for any of them,' put in Jack, picking up the plate of cakes. 'Can I tempt you, Anna?'

'Unfortunately, yes.' She sighed and chose a morsel smothered in chocolate.

Lucy did the same, but Kate shook her head, also refusing the brandy the men accepted.

'I'm driving, Jack.'

'So are you, dear,' George told his wife, who pouted girlishly, but made no protest.

'I wouldn't mind a nice little job like Kate's,' she declared, 'but George won't let me work.'

From the look on his face, Kate took it this was news to him.

'I never minded making coffee for my boss. In my opinion you just can't beat the personal touch,' Lucy went on relentlessly. 'The man I worked for was utterly devastated when I left to get married.'

'How about you, Kate?' said Ben, taking the chair nearest to her. 'Did your boss tear his hair when you resigned?'

She grinned at him. 'She paid far too much to her hairdresser to do that.'

'I'd hate to work for a woman,' said Lucy promptly.

'Kate worked *with* one, not for one,' said Anna, licking her fingers. 'She was Deputy Director of Human Resources by the time she resigned her London job.'

Lucy was silenced for a split second. 'Goodness, life must

be very different for you in a quiet town like this,' she said, regrouping.

Anna got up. 'If Kate will direct me, I need to find the ladies',' she announced.

'You'll have to ask Jack,' said Kate, smiling at her. 'I don't know where it is.'

'Really?' said Lucy, brightening. 'I'll come with you then, Anna.' She took Jack's arm, smiling up at him coquettishly as they left the room.

'You mustn't mind my wife, Kate,' said George kindly. 'She's got this boundless curiosity. She's probably nagging Jack to show her round the entire house right now.'

Kate gave him a friendly smile, and got up to take the coffee pot. 'I think I'll ask Molly for a refill. I do know where the kitchen is,' she told Ben as he opened the door for her.

Kate met Jack in the hall. 'I'm on my way to ask Molly for more coffee.'

'Good idea.' He grinned conspiratorially. 'How are you, Katie?'

'Bearing up,' she returned, rolling her eyes, and he laughed, smoothing a hand down her hair as she went on her way.

The kitchen was already tidy and the redoubtable Molly had a thermos of fresh coffee waiting to refill the silver pot.

'Mum can take it in.'

'Thank you,' said Kate gratefully. 'It was a fabulous meal, Molly,' she said as Hazel went off with the coffee. 'I hear you want to open a place of your own one day. When you do I'll be your first customer.'

'First dinner on the house then,' Molly assured her, beaming. 'You think the meal went down well tonight? I hope it wasn't too boring.'

'It was perfect. You must have seen the empty plates coming back! Mr Maitland had two helpings of everything. He said the apple pie was even better than his mother's.' Kate smiled at the sound of an imperious bark from the boot room.

'I think someone wants to say hello,' said Molly, and handed over a small dish of titbits. 'You can give Bran his treat, if you like—only mind that velvet.'

Kate received an enthusiastic greeting from Bran, who fussed over her in delight for a while, then wolfed down his goodies and went to stand pointedly at the outer door.

'You go back, Miss Durant. I'll let him out,' said Molly. 'The downstairs cloakroom is second on the right across the hall, by the way.'

Kate spent a few minutes there to marshal her forces, then went back to join the others.

'You've been a very long time,' commented Jack.

'I had a chat with Bran.'

'You were so long I poured the coffee,' said Lucy sweetly. 'Who's Bran?'

'My dog,' said Jack, and smiled as he took hairs from Kate's sleeve. 'You've been cuddling him.'

'Guilty as charged,' she said, and resumed her seat by Anna. 'How do you feel?' she said in an undertone, as Lucy fluttered round the men with the coffee pot.

'Fat,' said Anna ruefully. 'I shouldn't have eaten so much, but the food was so gorgeous I couldn't resist.'

'I relayed the praise to Molly.'

'Is Hazel her daughter?'

'Hazel is Molly's mother,' said Kate. 'How old is Molly, Jack? She looks like a schoolgirl.'

'Twenty-two and born old, according to her mother. There's a mature brain under that mane of blonde hair.'

Kate could practically see Lucy's brain ticking over. Blonde? Twenty-two?

'They say the way to a man's heart is through his stomach,' warned Lucy sharply. 'You'd better be careful, Jack. Maybe your Molly has designs on you.'

'You bet she has,' he said, unperturbed. 'She wants my backing when she opens her own restaurant.'

For the rest of the evening Jack did his best as host to keep the conversation general, but Lucy aimed barbs at Kate so often that at last George Beresford turned a look on his wife that plainly said 'enough' and she pouted and turned all her attention on Jack. Eventually Ben decided his wife looked tired and asked Lucy if she was ready to drive them home. Jack kept Kate firmly at his side while he received thanks for his hospitality. Anna and Ben kissed her goodnight, and George did the same, winning a sharp look from his wife, who kept her kissing strictly for her host. Jack stood in the open doorway as his guests hurried to the car under umbrellas, then went back inside to Kate with a sigh of relief.

'Thank you,' he said simply, running a hand through his hair.

'What for?'

'Just for being here.' He grimaced. 'I'll make sure I have a previous engagement when Lucy Beresford invites me to dinner again. I had a meal there once, purely because she wouldn't take no when I drove George home from a meeting.'

'She insisted you came to Anna's party as well,' Kate reminded him as they went back to the living room.

'For that alone I'm grateful to her,' admitted Jack, and put more logs on the fire. 'What can I give you to drink, Kate?'

'I should be going home.'

'Let's unwind for a bit first. Lucy gave you a hard time tonight. What got into the woman?'

'She resents me.' Kate kicked off her shoes to curl up in a corner of the sofa among the new cushions. 'Before Anna's party the Beresford dinner table was the only one in town you'd graced with your presence, so Lucy feels possessive where you're concerned. I'm afraid she took one look at me when she arrived tonight and jumped to the obvious conclusion. She was jealous.'

Jack groaned. 'Dammit, Kate, the woman's married to

someone I do business with, and has a couple of teenage children. Besides, I don't find her remotely attractive.'

'Maybe not, but Lucy lusts after you, Jack.'

'God!' He rubbed a hand over his chin, his eyes eloquent with distaste. 'Next time George needs a lift home I'll get him a taxi.'

'In the meantime I'll take you up on that offer of a drink. I'd like some tea.'

'You sit by the fire and I'll make it,' he said promptly.

'No, I'll come with you. I need a chat with Bran.'

'A fine thing,' said Jack as they crossed the hall, 'when a man is jealous of his own dog.'

Kate chuckled. 'He's a very handsome chap.'

Bran was wildly delighted to see them and after an interval of greeting and patting Kate perched on the table, swinging her feet, and Bran sat as near as he could get, gazing up at her in adoration.

'Just a teabag in a mug will do,' she told Jack as he filled the kettle. 'Make it strong. I need it.'

'I need something stronger than tea,' he said with feeling. 'I enjoyed my first shot at home entertaining, but next time I'll ask a different pair to make up the six.'

'You like Anna and Ben, then?'

'I do, very much. Though I get the feeling that Anna would cut my liver out with a blunt spoon if I hurt you in any way. I assume she knows our past history?'

'Afraid so.'

'Including Dawn?'

'Yes, but she won't broadcast it.'

'She doesn't have to. The story of my marriage and divorce is well known.'

'Do you mind?'

'I was young enough to mind quite at lot at first, but I got over it.' Jack turned to look at her. 'Getting over you, Kate, was a damn sight harder. And my way of coping was a hard work no play lifestyle that did wonders for the company but nothing for me socially. At least,' he added candidly, 'not until we opened the London office. But that's all in the past. From now on I'll do more entertaining at home.' He touched a hand to her cheek as he handed her the tea. 'It felt so right to see you at the other end of my table, Katie.'

She sipped carefully, trying to bypass the lump in her throat.

'Did it feel right to you?' he asked quietly.

Kate looked up into his intent eyes. 'Yes, Jack it did. But you can't expect me to play hostess every time you entertain.'

'Why not?'

'I'm not getting into that kind of arrangement with you.'

'You're afraid of what people might think?'

'I'm more concerned with what you might think, Jack.' Kate put down her half empty mug and slid off the table. 'Time I went home.'

Jack caught her by the elbow, his touch burning through the velvet. 'Stay.'

'No,' she said flatly.

'I meant long enough to drink your tea,' he said impatiently. 'Come and sit by the fire for a few minutes. Bran can come as chaperon if you like.'

'Jack, I want to go home,' she said with such vehemence that he released her and went from the room. She pushed a hand through her hair, blinking hard, and crossed the room to tear a sheet from a roll of paper kitchen towel.

'Katie!' said Jack behind her.

She buried her face in the paper towel, but he took her by the shoulders and turned her round until her face was against his shirt. Jack smoothed a hand over her hair and held her until the tears stopped He left her for a moment, then put his arms round her again.

At last she drew away and scrubbed the sodden paper over her face. 'Sorry,' she said thickly.

'So am I. I can't handle it when you cry.' Jack smoothed a strand of damp hair from her forehead. 'I've brought your things if you really must go now.'

'Right.' She sniffed inelegantly. 'Where's Bran?'

'He couldn't handle it either. I put him in the boot room.' Kate looked up at Jack in remorse. 'Poor Bran.'

'Not poor Jack?'

'That, too—sorry about your shirt,' she added hoarsely, eyeing the mascara streaks and sodden patches on his chest.

'The shirt will wash.' Jack took her hand. 'Stay until you feel better, Kate. I'll make more tea, and we'll take Bran in by the fire until you're in good enough shape to drive home.'

'All right,' she said listlessly. 'But I'll just wash my face first.'

A few minutes later, curled up in a corner of the sofa with Bran at her feet and a fresh mug of tea steaming at her elbow, Kate felt a little better. Jack settled beside her to finish his brandy, long legs stretched out in front of him.

'I can guess why you cried,' he said quietly.

She gave him a narrowed, sidelong glance. 'Can you?'

'I could have cried myself. This was how it should have been all along, the two of us as a couple, entertaining friends to dinner. And it's how it would have been if I hadn't made such a hellish mess of things.' He turned to her in sudden urgency. 'But it could be like that in future. I want you back, Kate. I've tried to be patient, not rush things, but we've wasted so much of our lives already.'

'No!' Kate tore her eyes away from the demand in Jack's, and shook her head. 'One can't go back.'

'But you did *come* back,' he said quickly, his eyes triumphant. 'And you knew from the magazine article that I was still here.'

'Also still married, as far as I knew,' she reminded him. 'But the fact that you're single again doesn't change anything. It would be disastrous for us to get back together.'

'Why?' he demanded.

'First and last and most important, I have responsibility for Joanna.' Kate turned her head and met his eyes. 'And secondly, Jack, I'm not the girl who was so hopelessly in love with you all those years ago. We're both responsible adults now, so if you want me as a friend, fine. But I don't want you as a lover.'

Jack's eyes turned to steel. 'I don't believe that. Last night your body responded to me just the way it used to—until your mind slammed on the brakes.'

'That was chemistry. It doesn't mean anything. You could always make me respond, Jack.' Her mouth tightened. 'You obviously had the same effect on Dawn.'

'Which is the real obstacle,' he said harshly.

'Only one of the many.' Kate stood up. 'Time I went home. Where did you put my boots?'

'In the kitchen. I'll fetch them.'

Kate bent to stroke the dog, blinking when she felt tears threaten again. She was tired, that was all. She'd been a fool to finish painting today after a virtually sleepless night. And, though she'd enjoyed the evening in some ways, in others it had been a strain, due partly to Lucy Beresford and her sniping, but not entirely. Jack was right. At the dinner table she *had* felt regret for what might have been. She sighed, and as though tuned in to her mood, Bran got up to push his head against her thigh in comfort.

When Jack returned he waited in silence while she changed her shoes, then held her raincoat for her and went through the hall to open the main door. He frowned at the sheeting rain, but before he could put up the golf umbrella his phone rang, and he closed the door on the deluge to answer it.

'No, Ben, she was just leaving.' He listened intently for a moment, looking at Kate. 'Sounds bad. I'll hand you over. You'd better tell her yourself.'

Kate snatched the phone from him. 'Ben! Is something wrong with Anna?'

'No, love, nothing like that. She's worried to death about *you*. Thank God you haven't left yet. The roads are flooded pretty much all the way from Mill House into town. We only just made it home in George's Range Rover, so you wouldn't have a hope in your car—' He broke off. 'Hang on, Kate, Anna wants a word.'

'Tell Jack either he must drive you or you stay the night,' said Anna fiercely. 'Don't even think of trying to drive yourself. Lucy had hysterics when we hit the first flood water, so I had to take over.'

'But you're pregnant!'

'There were loads of police about and the men were over the limit, so there was no choice. It was a slow journey, but with Ben as co-driver I was fine. But that was in a four wheel drive, Kate. Let me talk to Jack.'

'Anna—'

'No arguing; hand the phone back.'

Kate gave Jack the phone and stood watching his face as he spoke to Anna. At last he said goodnight and snapped the phone shut.

'I'm sorry, Kate. I can't drive you as I'm already over the limit.' He gave a wry shrug. 'No help for it, I'm afraid. You'll have to spend the night in my guest room.'

CHAPTER EIGHT

KATE'S first instinct was to refuse point blank. Then common
sense kicked in. It was her only option. 'Thank you,' she said
reluctantly. 'Sorry to be a nuisance.'

'Not at all,' said Jack politely. 'I'll show you where to
sleep.' He ordered Bran to his bed, and opened the door into
the hall.

In silence Kate followed him up the white-painted staircase
to a room no bigger than her bedroom in Park Crescent. The
furniture was plain and contemporary, and the curtains and
bedcovers were white but, unlike the rest of the house, the
room was painted a creamy shade of yellow.

'Attractive,' said Kate, so tired by this time she could
hardly stand straight.

'Sherbet,' said Jack.

She stared at him blankly.

'You're up on paint colours, Kate. This is Sherbet.'

'Oh, right.'

'The bathroom—a very small one, is behind the door over
there,' he informed her. 'I hope you sleep well.'

'Thank you.'

Jack said goodnight and closed the door and, with a sigh
Kate collected some hangers from the wardrobe and went into
the bathroom. It was small, as Jack warned, but wonderfully
warm and fully equipped with everything a guest could need,
best of all a towelling dressing gown. She undressed hurriedly
and got into it, then hung her suit and camisole on the shower
rail, rinsed out her underwear and arranged it on the radiator.
She was squeezing toothpaste on to a brand-new toothbrush
when Jack knocked on the bedroom door.

Kate opened it to find him holding out one of his white T-shirts.

'I thought you might need this.'

'Thank you. I borrowed the dressing gown,' she added unnecessarily.

'So I see. Goodnight again.'

'Goodnight, Jack.'

Kate brushed her teeth, washed her face again, and did what she could with her hair. At last, almost dizzy with nervous strain and fatigue, she turned back the bedcovers, took off the dressing gown and laid it on a chair. She pulled the big T-shirt over her head and turned off the bedside lamps, then slid thankfully into bed. Bed and breakfast after all, was her last waking thought.

She woke with a start, face wet and heart pounding at the sound of Jack's frantic voice as he shook her gently. Her eyes widened in horror as she took in her surroundings. She was downstairs in the hall and Bran was barking frantically somewhere. Oh, God, she thought. Not now, not here!

'I'm so s-sorry,' she said through chattering teeth.

Jack slid out of his dressing gown, his face haggard as he wrapped it round her. 'Put that on while I sort the dog out. Don't move an inch until I get back.'

Kate tied the cord with shaking hands and found a handkerchief in one of the dressing gown pockets. She mopped her face and had composed herself slightly by the time Jack came back.

'I left my bedroom door ajar, which is why I heard you crying,' he said grimly. 'You scared the hell out of me when I found you halfway down the stairs. But when you looked right through me my hair really stood on end. Tears were streaming down your face but your eyes were totally blank. Once I realised you were sleepwalking I was afraid to wake you, so I went down beside you, step by step, ready to grab you if you fell.'

'I never fall,' she said hoarsely.

Jack's eyes narrowed. 'You do this often?'

'Occasionally, in times of stress.' She shrugged. 'It's my own fault. I hardly slept last night after—after you left, and then I worked all day to finish painting. I was tired even before I arrived. Lucy was bitchy, and I got uptight with you over times past and on top of that I couldn't go home because of the floods and—' She hesitated, biting her lip.

'And the final straw was spending the night in Bluebeard's castle. So in your subconscious you tried to escape,' said Jack grimly.

She shook her head. 'It's nothing to do with this house, Jack, or escape.'

'When did the sleepwalking start?'

'Ages ago. But by the time I moved in with Anna I was more or less over it.'

His face hardened into bitter lines. 'But one hour in bed in *my* house and you wanted out.'

Kate's teeth began to chatter, and Jack's eyes darkened with contrition. 'You're freezing. I'll get you back to bed, then make you some more tea. Give me your hand.'

She let him lead her up the stairs, feeling contrite herself when she realised that Jack's only garment was a pair of boxers. 'You must be cold, too.'

'Only with fright.' He took in a deep breath. 'Once my pulse rate drops below a hundred again I'll be fine.'

When they reached the spare room Jack switched on the light and stared at the bed. The quilt and pillows were on the floor, the fitted bottom sheets snarled in a crumpled heap, and he swore under his breath when he picked up the pillows.

'When you cry you really cry. These are damp.' He turned to her and undid the dressing gown to touch the T-shirt. 'Hell, this is, too. I'll bring you another one with the clean sheets—' He stopped suddenly and shot her a look. 'Are you likely to do this again tonight?'

'I don't *know*,' she said miserably.

'Have you done any sleepwalking in Park Crescent?'

'No.' Not yet.

He looked at her searchingly. 'Did it start when we broke up? Is that why you won't let me get close again?'

'Part of it.' She shrugged. 'Stress acts in different ways on different people—migraine, anxiety attacks and so on. In my case it's sleepwalking. But I hadn't done it for years until Liz and Robert were killed. Then I had the row with Rupert and it happened again.'

'And I caused this tonight by pestering you to come back to me,' Jack said harshly. He picked up the towelling dressing gown and held it out. 'Go in the bathroom and put this on while I strip the bed. You need sleep.'

Kate splashed cold water on her swollen eyes, then went back into the bedroom.

Jack looked up from the linen he was bundling together, his eyes strained. 'I hope to God you don't go walkabout again.'

'If I could promise not to, I would,' she said unhappily. 'I hate doing it, Jack. Waking up somewhere else is pretty scary, believe me.'

'I do.' He stood very still, every muscle in his bare chest taut, then pulled on the dressing gown and tied the cord with unnecessary force. 'There's a remedy. For tonight, at least.'

'Knockout drops?' she said, trying to smile.

'No.' Jack eyed her in appeal. 'Look, Kate, I make this offer with the best of intentions, so don't panic. Come and sleep in my room. That way we might both get some sleep. At least I'd know if you took off again.' He smiled a little. 'I promise faithfully to keep to my side of the bed. It's big enough to sleep four at a pinch, so no problem with over-crowding.'

Not trusting her voice, she nodded slowly in assent.

The master bedroom was at the other end of the upper

corridor and the bed was vast, as Jack had promised. He turned back the covers on the far side, told her to get in, then searched in a chest between the tall windows. He tossed a thick white sweatshirt on the bed for her, then made for the door.

'Where are you going?' she demanded.

'To make you that tea. You're shivering, Kate. For God's sake, get into bed and try to get warm.'

Kate took off the dressing gown, pulled on the warm fleecy shirt, and slid under the covers, teeth chattering. This was probably a big mistake, but it was better than waking up in some other part of the house again, scaring Jack and waking Bran into the bargain.

Jack came back with a tray and put it on the chest. He ordered Kate to sit up, propped pillows behind her and then brought her a mug of tea. 'I added a spoonful of something medicinal,' he told her. 'We need it.'

'Thank you,' she said, subdued, and sipped gratefully, feeling the warmth spread through her as the brandy and scalding tea did their work. When Jack slid in beside her with his own drink she shot him a rueful glance. 'One way and another, you won't forget your first official dinner party.'

'True.' He grinned suddenly. 'If Lucy Beresford could only see us now!'

'She'd be wild with jealousy.'

'But certainly wouldn't picture us drinking tea together! You'd better look out, Kate. I think she's also jealous of your relationship with Anna Maitland,' he warned.

She pulled a face. 'I'll watch my back on two counts, then.'

'If she gives you any trouble, let me know,' said Jack grimly. 'I'll get George to sort her out. He may look easy-going but there's steel underneath that sense of humour.'

'I saw that for myself. I like him.'

'You like Ben Maitland, too.'

'I do. From the first day Anna introduced me to him I felt

I'd known him all my life,' Kate explained. 'And he's great with Joanna. She adores them both, and she's thrilled to bits about the baby.'

'Ben's a lucky man,' said Jack, and took her mug away. 'Time you went to sleep, Kate.'

'It seems hardly worth it.'

'A couple of hours' rest would do you good, so I'm putting out the light.'

'Goodnight then, Jack. And thank you.'

'No thanks necessary. Now give me your hand and try to relax.'

Kate did as he said and slid down in the bed, smiling when she found there was almost a foot of space between them. But the hard, warm grasp of Jack's outstretched hand gave her such a sense of security she felt herself relax, muscle by muscle, as she slid into mercifully dreamless sleep.

CHAPTER NINE

KATE woke slowly to pale daylight filtering below the Roman blinds and the discovery that Jack was close against her, his arm heavy on her waist. At some point in the night he'd moved close, holding her spoon fashion. She could feel his breath on her neck and kept perfectly still until a slight movement told her Jack was awake. She smiled to herself. It was a new experience to wake up with him like this. In their youth their sessions in bed had been all too brief, and never overnight.

'I know you're not asleep,' he whispered, and moved away to leave space between them. She turned over, smiling as she faced him, and he brushed a stray lock of hair back from her forehead. 'We've never woken up together before, Katie.'

'I was just thinking that.'

His eyes held hers. Seen at this range in the morning light, she could make out little flecks of silver in the dark-rimmed grey irises. 'I've never done this with anyone else, either,' he said casually.

Kate's eyebrows shot up. 'You must have done!'

He shook his head. 'During various encounters over the years I never stayed the night.'

'You're forgetting Dawn.'

'As if either of us could ever do that!' he retorted. 'Just for the record, when we were married Dawn and I didn't sleep together.'

Kate stared in disbelief. 'If she was expecting your child you must have done some time!'

'Before the wedding our few encounters were brief and to the point,' he said with brutal frankness. 'Dawn's room was over the garage block at the pub. It had a separate entrance via a fire escape. She began asking me up there for coffee after her shift at the bar, but at first I politely declined. Then one night I felt so damn miserable I caved in. But I never stayed until her father closed the pub, let alone the night.'

Kate eyed him curiously. 'And after you were married?'

Jack's mouth turned down. 'The bride felt so ill at the register office she couldn't cope with the meal her mother had organised. Only Dad and her parents were there, so as soon as the knot was tied the newlyweds went straight to the flat in Gloucester Road and Dawn went to bed. I spent the afternoon doing paperwork, and my wedding night watching television on the sofa in the sitting room. Next day I bought a bed for the spare room and slept there from then on.'

'Was she unwell all the time then?'

'Pretty much. Her mother was a godsend. She came in every day, did laundry and housework and left meals for me. I went back to the flat in time for dinner every evening, but I ate alone because Dawn couldn't stand the sight of food. I sat with her afterwards, but—' He paused, rubbing his chin. 'To be blunt, conversation was an uphill struggle at the best of times, so we just sat staring at the television, or I made paperwork an excuse and escaped to the spare room. Then one night she woke in pain, and I rushed her off to hospital. You know the rest.' Jack kissed Kate's nose and slid out of bed. 'I'm hungry. Stay there and I'll bring you some breakfast.'

'Certainly not, I'll come down!'

Jack pushed her gently against the pillows. 'Rest for a bit, you look tired. I'll throw Bran out and then bring up a tray. Humour me, Kate.' He pulled up the blinds, collected some clothes and went into the bathroom. When he emerged in a heavy sweater and workmanlike cords, he was a little heavy around the eyes but otherwise looked none the worse for his disturbed night.

'Ten minutes,' he promised.

When the door closed behind him Kate made a dash for the bathroom. Longing to take a shower, she contented herself with washing her face and rubbing toothpaste over her teeth with her finger. She rinsed with cold water, borrowed Jack's comb then tidied the bed. She got into it and leaned back against stacked pillows as she noted every detail of the masculine room, which held no clutter of any kind other than a few books on the bedside tables. Except for the two antique chests, Jack had obviously bought his bedroom furniture from the same source as everything else in the house.

Jack arrived soon afterwards with a tray he set down on the low chest at the foot of the bed. He handed her a glass of orange juice, then gave her a fork and a linen napkin and put a large serving plate between them on the bed.

'Heavens, Jack,' she said, eyeing the pile of toast surrounding a big mound of scrambled eggs. 'I can't eat all this.'

'Good, because half of it is for me. No room for individual plates on the tray. Don't worry,' he said, grinning. 'I've got my own fork.'

Kate chuckled, and asked about the furniture when Jack sat beside her with the plate between them.

'The firm concentrates on quality rather than mass production and made everything individually to my specifications. After their coverage in the article the orders came flooding in, so we're all happy,' said Jack. 'I believe in patronising local tradesmen. Come on, eat up,' he added, 'you're lagging behind.'

When the plate was empty Jack got up and filled two mugs, then returned to his place on the bed.

'I made the coffee while Bran was out doing the necessary, then decanted it into Molly's insulated jug. I like my coffee red-hot.'

'I remember,' said Kate, sipping cautiously.

Jack leaned back at the foot of the bed, eyeing her in wry

amusement. 'I've thought of having you in this bed right from the moment we met up again, Kate, but never in quite these circumstances.'

'I bet,' she said dryly, and smiled. 'But this is nice, just the same, Jack.'

'It is,' he agreed. 'Friendship with you isn't really such hard work.'

'Even after the fright I gave you last night?'

He frowned. 'What happens when you sleepwalk in Park Crescent?'

'I haven't so far.'

'How do you know?'

Kate drank some of her coffee. 'For obvious reasons I'm always barefoot when I wander. If my feet are clean when I wake up I'm in the clear. And, contrary to belief, sleepwalkers don't drift round like ghosts; they knock things over and bump into furniture. So if everything's in its place I know I've stayed in bed all night. Besides,' she added, 'even if I found the key and unbolted the front door in my sleep I'd wake up pretty quickly when the alarm went off.'

'True.' Jack looked relieved. 'You've had that kind of security everywhere you've lived?'

Kate nodded soberly. 'Robert installed it in their place, and I had it done in Anna's flat when I moved there. David's loft was already like a fortress, so no problem, but I did the necessary when I went to live alone in Notting Hill, and again before I moved into Park Crescent.'

Jack looked thoughtful as he finished his coffee. 'You might not get out of the actual house there, but those stairs are hellish steep. You could fall and break something—like your neck.'

Kate shook her head. 'There were stairs in the Sutton household, but I stayed in one piece.'

'How often did it happen there?'

Her eyes dropped. 'More than I liked. As you can appre-

ciate, it was a bad time for me when I was first living with
them in London. But it only happened once after I moved into
Anna's flat.'

'Did she know about it beforehand?'

'Of course. I had to tell her that when I applied to share.
But Anna wasn't fazed. Her brother was captain of the first
eleven at his school and used to walk in his sleep before
important cricket matches. He'd get out of bed in the dormitory with his bat, and shape up to an invisible wicket.'

Jack grinned. 'That must have been fun for his mates.'

'Apparently they just bowled a few balls to him and he
went back to bed.'

'You're making that up!'

'I'm not. Nick Travers told me that himself.'

Jack chuckled as he put their mugs on the tray, then shot
her a questioning look. 'Are you having lunch with the
Maitlands today?'

Kate shook her head. 'I'm having supper with them during
the week instead.'

He looked at her speculatively. 'And you've finished your
painting, so what are you going to do today?'

She shrugged. 'Nothing much.'

'Then you can do that here with me, Kate.'

'I'll have to if the floodwater hasn't gone down,' she reminded him.

'So you will,' he said with satisfaction. 'Until I'm sure it's
safe for you to drive, you're my captive. We can share leftovers for lunch.' He smiled. 'It's a fine day, so we could take
Bran for a walk first to work up an appetite.'

'All right, you've persuaded me.' Kate had intended to say
yes right from the start, but Jack didn't have to know that.
'May I have a shower, please?'

'Of course. I'll make more coffee when you come down.'

Kate hurried to the pretty spare room, gathered up the
sheets and removed the covers from the duvet and pillows

and folded everything into a neat pile. After her shower she put on Jack's sweatshirt in preference to her thin camisole, pulled on her boots, used a lipstick, dragged a comb through her hair and hurried down to the kitchen with the bundle of laundry.

Bran came to meet her in such joyous welcome she scratched his ears and dropped a kiss on his head.

'How about me?' asked Jack.

Kate grinned. 'You want me to scratch *your* ears?'

'I meant the kiss.'

'OK. Bend down, then.'

Jack bent his head and Kate stood on tiptoe to kiss his cheek.

'Is that the best you can do?' he demanded.

'Bran didn't complain.'

Jack snatched the bundle from her, dumped it on the floor and pulled her into his arms to kiss her squarely on her protesting mouth, while the dog frisked round them, obviously thinking it was some kind of game. 'I like *that* kind of kiss,' Jack informed her as he let her go.

'I'll make a note of it,' Kate said breathlessly, and tore a sheet from the roll of kitchen paper. 'Here, lose the lipstick. That shade just isn't you.'

Jack grinned and scrubbed at his mouth. 'Come and sit down. I've made coffee.'

'I'll deal with this lot first. Where's your washing machine?'

'Leave it. Molly will do it.'

'Certainly not, I will,' Kate said firmly. 'And if you show me where you keep your spare bed linen I'll make the bed, too.'

'You never used to be so bossy,' he complained, and took the laundry into the boot room, which was fitted with every conceivable aid for washing, drying and ironing, along with a refrigerator and vast freezer, and floor to ceiling cupboards for food storage.

Kate smiled as she saw the small folding stepladder near the tall cupboards. 'That's for Molly, I assume. This is very impressive, Jack, but why a boot room?'

'This end of the house contained the actual living quarters for the mill owner, with a scullery here where the boots were cleaned by the boy employed for the job.'

Once the washing machine was in action Jack insisted Kate had some coffee before she put clean linen on the spare bed.

He perched on the corner of the table, one foot swinging. 'In fact, I've got a better idea. I've started the fire in the living room and even tidied up a bit, so you can lie on the sofa there and read the Sunday papers with Bran while *I* do the bed.'

She smiled warmly. 'An offer I can't refuse! Thank you, Jack.'

In the morning sunshine, with flames leaping in the fireplace and two brand-new paperback novels placed beside the Sunday papers on the rosewood table, the living room looked very inviting. Bran deserted Kate instantly to lie on the rug in front of the fire, and she added more logs, bent to stroke the dog, and then curled up in a corner of the sofa. She read a few headlines in the papers but, unable to resist any longer, picked up one of the books, a thriller she'd intended to buy the moment it was out in the bookshops.

The story was riveting from the first page. But almost at once the warmth of the fire combined with her disturbed night to add weight to her eyelids and soon she put the book down and lay back against the new cushions. She stirred to the touch of familiar lips on hers and her mouth curved in response as her eyes opened on a look in Jack's which turned her heart over. He stretched out beside her and caught her close, and Kate felt his heart hammer against her as his mouth crushed hers in a kiss that went on and on until neither could breathe and his lips left hers to cover her face and throat with kisses as he slid his hands up her ribs. He pushed the sweatshirt up until his lips found her breasts and she gave a low, gasping moan as he held her in an embrace that threatened to crush her ribs.

'When I woke up this morning,' he said hoarsely, 'I wanted this so much I could barely breathe.'

'I wanted it too,' she said huskily, and buried her face against his neck.

'I wish I'd known that.' He turned her face up to his. 'Tell me about your dream last night. What sent you running head-long down the stairs?'

'As usual I was looking for you, but never finding you.' She put a hand to his cheek. 'I didn't need much persuasion to sleep in your bed. I wanted to break my dream.'

Jack sat up and pulled her up with him in the crook of his arm. 'If I helped with that I think I deserve a reward.'

'You want me to put on lunch?'

'I'm hungry for you, not lunch. Come back to bed with me.'

'How about Bran?'

'He can stay in his own bed.' Jack got up and held out his hand, a look of such blazing relief in his eyes when she grasped it, she hugged him close when he pulled her to her feet.

I want this so much, Kate thought as they went upstairs together. I need it to make up for all those times when I searched for Jack in my dreams and could never find him.

'If I were the hero in a romance,' Jack said huskily, 'I would have swept you up and carried you up to bed, but it's a fair trip from the living room up the stairs. But,' he added, picking her up once they reached the top corridor, 'I can manage it from here.'

Kate gave a breathless laugh as he strode the short distance to his room. Once inside he kicked the door shut, kissed her until she was even more breathless, and laid her on the bed.

'I've never stopped loving you, Kate,' he said, leaning over her. 'You may find that hard to believe, but it's the truth.'

'Is it, Jack?' she said quietly. 'There were long years when my feelings for you were more like hate.'

'I don't blame you.' He stretched out beside her and held her close, his cheek on her hair. 'I don't blame Elizabeth, either.'

Kate stiffened and turned in his arms. 'Liz? What do you mean?'

'She never told you, then.'

'Told me what?'

'I went to London to see you the minute my divorce was final. Your sister had already moved to a different house by then, but I persuaded the new owners to let me have the Suttons' forwarding address and went straight there.' Jack laid his forehead against hers, eyes closed.

'What happened, Jack?'

'Elizabeth wouldn't let me through the door. She said you had a new job and had moved out to share a flat.' His mouth twisted. 'No matter how hard I pleaded she wouldn't give me your telephone number or tell me where you lived. She said you wanted nothing more to do with me, ever, and slammed the door in my face.'

Kate burrowed closer. 'Oh, *Jack*—she never told me.'

'It was at that point I gave up on relationships. Eventually I heard you were living with some banker in Docklands.' Jack kissed her fiercely. 'I wanted to kill him.'

Kate's eyes flashed. 'Now you know how I felt about Dawn—and you.'

'You wanted to kill me?'

'Yes. Very slowly.'

'Do you still want to kill me?' he asked, and took her ear-lobe between his teeth. 'Because if you don't let me make love to you very soon you'll get your wish.'

Kate gave a smothered laugh. 'That's the last thing I want, Jack.'

He pulled her closer. 'What do you want then, my darling?'

Instead of words Kate gave him a slow, explicit smile which won her a kiss she responded to with such fervour he lifted her from the bed and stood her on her feet to undress her with unsteady hands, fighting to go slowly rather than tear off her clothes. When she was naked to the waist he began kissing his way down her throat to her breasts, lingering on nipples that rose erect and hard in response to his lips and tongue. But when he reached for her zip she shook her head.

'You too,' she ordered, and Jack began pulling off his clothes. But, before he could get naked, Kate had undressed herself and burrowed under the covers. She turned them back a little and held out her arms. 'Hold me, please.'

Jack dived under the quilt, exerting every iota of will-power he possessed to keep from pulling her beneath him and taking swift, desperate possession of her in the way he'd wanted since he first set eyes on her again. He drew in a deep, shuddering breath and closed his eyes as he kissed her gently, teasing her tongue with his and nibbling gently on her bottom lip. He pressed kisses all over her face while his hands stroked and smoothed, and gained his reward when he felt the tense, slender body begin to relax.

'No rush,' he whispered in her ear. 'I want to enjoy every little inch of you.'

Kate felt as though every bone in her body was slowly melting as Jack kissed her and caressed her with a languorous lack of haste that made her impatient at last for the heat and hunger she'd seen in his eyes before she dived into bed. But at last his caresses grew more urgent, his lips and tongue and grazing teeth sending fiery sensation from the tips of her breasts to the part which melted in hot liquid response deep down inside her. She thrust her hips against him and felt a surge of triumph as his breath caught and his muscles grew taught under the hands she dug into his shoulders. She gave a husky little moan as his caressing fingers slid between her thighs to find the small, hidden bud that rose, tumescent, to the caresses which sent her wild with almost unbearable pleasure, and in answer to her gasped, broken pleading he nudged her thighs apart with his knee. He raised his head and their eyes met and held as he took slow, sure possession of her at last. They stayed as still as their rapid breathing allowed for a moment, then began to move together, savouring every last nuance of sensation as he slid home and withdrew, then repeated the process a little faster and harder each time, their mutual fire stoked higher and higher with every stroke until the rhythm of their loving rose to frenzy and at last the climax engulfed them in heart-stopping release.

'We never achieved that in the past,' Kate whispered a long time later.

Jack raised the face he'd buried in her hair and lifted an eyebrow. 'That?' he inquired. 'A small word for a mind altering experience.'

She chuckled. 'I meant the timing. We were sometimes out of step back then.'

'You mean I was so hot for you I sometimes lost control,' he said wryly. 'I felt the same this time. It took every scrap of will-power I possessed to keep from ravishing you the moment I laid you on the bed.'

'Ravishing is good,' she assured him. 'A woman likes to know she's desirable.' Kate's eyes clouded. 'It was a long time before I felt even passably attractive after you left me for Dawn.'

He winced, and moved away a fraction. 'I suppose this banker of yours helped with that.'

'Yes, he did. But it was never like this with David.' Kate looked at him steadily. 'Nor with anyone else, Jack.'

He pulled her back into his arms and kissed her. 'God, I've missed you, Katie.'

They lay in each other's arms for a long, quiet interval, but at last Jack kissed her again and slid out of bed.

'Let's eat,' he said, getting dressed.

'You go on down. I'll follow you in a minute.'

He grinned as he collected her clothes. 'I've watched you dress before.'

'But not lately and not today.' Kate pulled the quilt up to her chin.

Jack gave her a threatening look as he strolled to the door. 'Ten minutes or I come and get you.'

Once the door closed behind him Kate slid out of bed, picked up her clothes and raced into the bathroom. Ten minutes later she met Jack in the hall.

'I was just coming to look for you.'

Kate patted her midriff. 'I'm hungry. I didn't think I would be after that huge breakfast, but I am.'

Jack grinned. 'Making love always did give you an appetite. You were so skinny in those days it always amazed me that you ate as much as I did—more sometimes.'

'Lucky metabolism.'

Bran came wagging in joyful greeting as they went into the kitchen. Kate made a big fuss of him, then inspected the kitchen table with approval. Jack had put out the remains of the ham with a bowl of ripe red tomatoes, a loaf of Molly's wholemeal bread and the platter of cheese from the night before.

'I gave Bran one of his treats to celebrate,' said Jack as he began to carve the ham.

'Celebrate what?' said Kate innocently.

He gave her a look which curled her toes. 'You know damn well!'

Kate enjoyed the meal far more than the dinner of the evening before. They brought each other up to date on their taste in books, Jack reported on the progress of his current project and Kate talked about her clients and the trip she was making the following weekend to see Joanna.

When her phone rang Kate touched a finger to her lips and showed Jack the identity of her caller as she went out into the hall. 'Hi, Anna.'

'Did Jack drive you home last night?'

'No. I stayed the night in his guest room.'

'Thank goodness for that. I was worried sick. Look, I must apologise for Lucy. She was an absolute cow to you last night.'

'Not your fault. She's obviously got a great big crush on Jack.'

'I didn't realise just how great big it was. She was so cock-a-hoop about being invited, but then she found you in possession, stunning in your black velvet against all that whiteness, and Lucy was jealous as hell.'

'You looked stunning yourself. But did Lucy borrow her dress from her daughter by any chance?'

'No way—Rose wouldn't be seen dead in something like that.' Anna chuckled. 'Lucy was—and is—a fan of *Sex and the City*, hence the dress and matching toenails. She owns the entire series on DVD and watches for hours when George is away.'

'That explains a lot. But I don't remember her looking like that at your party.'

'You were too stunned by meeting Jack again to notice.'

'True. But never mind Lucy; is everything all right with baby after your epic drive home last night?'

'Absolutely fine. Anxious Daddy cooked lunch today and I'm putting my feet up this afternoon.'

'Good. Keep doing that. I'll talk to you tomorrow.'

Kate turned to see Jack laughing in the doorway. 'Did you eavesdrop?'

'Every word. You were discussing Lucy Beresford's dress, I take it.'

'Guilty! Girls will be girls.' She explained about the television series which Jack, as expected, had never seen, so wasn't much the wiser.

'Are you saying she got herself up like that purely on my account?'

Kate grinned. 'It certainly wasn't on mine!'

Jack's mouth twisted in distaste. 'Even if I were fool enough to play around with the wife of a friend I like and respect, it would not be Lucy Beresford.'

'Sensible man!'

He sighed. 'But somehow I have to make that clear to the lady, and at the same time keep George as a friend.'

'Tricky,' agreed Kate.

Jack's patience suddenly ran out. 'You could help me with that.'

'How?' she said, eyes narrowed.

He took her hands in his. 'Darling, I meant to wait a while before I brought it up, but surely you can see what I'm getting at?'

'No, I can't.'

'The best way out of the dilemma is to acquire a wife of my own—you, Kate.'

She stared at him. 'Are you serious?'

'It's not the sort of thing one says as a joke! We've wasted too much of our lives apart already, so for God's sake let's get married, Kate.' He waited, his eyes darkening at her lack of response. 'I see. You obviously don't care for the idea. Should I have gone down on one knee?'

'The answer would still have been no, Jack.'

He dropped her hands, turned his back and strode into the living room to stand at the far windows, his back turned.

Kate followed as far as the fireplace. She waited quietly until he faced her, and forced herself to meet the ice in his eyes.

'Did you plan this?' he asked, in a voice so quiet and cutting she winced.

'What do you mean?'

'When you met me again, and found I was divorced,' he went on in that same deadly quiet voice, 'did you see a golden opportunity for revenge?'

'Unlike you to be melodramatic, Jack,' she said with distaste. 'Anyway, you're wrong.'

'I don't think so.' He thrust his hands in his pockets and strolled towards her, lover transformed into menacing stranger. 'The more I think about it, the more I'm convinced that you've had this in mind from the moment we met up again. String him along, play hard to get, and then show him what he's been missing. And put the cherry on top by turning him down flat when he proposes. Did that feel good, Kate?' he demanded.

She shook her head silently.

'So now what? Don't tell me you want us to be good friends!' He gave a mirthless bark of laughter. 'At this moment in time, Kate Durant, I don't feel friendly at all.'

'I can see that, and I'm sorry for it.' She turned away, unable to hold that hard, implacable gaze a moment longer. 'It's my fault. I shared your room last night because after the sleepwalking episode I was scared to stay on my own.'

'That was last night,' said Jack grimly. 'But it was broad daylight when we made love this morning. You were wide awake when we walked all the way upstairs to my bedroom, Kate. You had ample opportunity to say no along the way. So why the hell didn't you?'

She eyed him in surprise. 'Surely it's obvious. I wanted to make love with you—simple as that.'

'Why?'

'Curiosity, nostalgia, lust—take your pick. I wanted to find out if it would still be good with you.'

'And was it?' he asked casually, as though her answer was unimportant.

But Kate knew it wasn't. She could see a telltale pulse throbbing at the corner of his clenched mouth. 'It was miraculous, Jack. I told you that. Better than with anyone else. But it makes no difference. Even if you're still of the same mind…and, by the look on your face, I doubt that—I can't marry you.' She hesitated. 'We could be lovers again, though, surely?'

Jack gave her a flaying look, then bent to put more logs on the fire. 'You mean you love the sex, but you don't want me as a husband?'

'Something like that.'

He turned expressionless eyes on her. 'Did it give you a buzz to tell me that, Kate? Did it make up for your hurt when I married Dawn?'

'You have no idea how much you hurt me,' she said with sudden passion. 'One of my reasons for turning you down is to avoid similar hurt in future.'

His mouth twisted. 'A pity you didn't let me know that sooner.'

'A great pity,' she agreed.

'What are the other reasons?'

'Pretty obvious ones. When I inherited the house I found a new job, made a home here for Joanna and me—'

'And there's no room for a husband in your tidy little life,' Jack said harshly. He looked at her objectively, as though seeing her for the first time. 'When we met up again I thought you'd hardly changed at all. I was wrong. You've grown hard, Kate.'

'I prefer to think of it as mature. But I agree I'm not the malleable little girl you once knew.'

'Malleable!' He laughed again. 'That's a joke. Nothing I could do or say back then changed your mind about a job in London.'

'True. But marrying someone else by way of retaliation was a bit extreme, even for you, Jack,' she flung at him.

They looked at each other in hostile silence for a while, then Jack took the phone from his pocket, excused himself politely and went out. Kate stayed by the fire, staring down into the flames as her heartbeat gradually slowed to normal. The odd, abrupt proposal had taken her by surprise. She just hadn't seen it coming. If she had, maybe she could have deflected it somehow without alienating Jack so completely.

Jack came back into the room with Bran padding after him, and Kate bent to fondle the dog's ears to hide the sudden tears of bitter regret in her eyes.

'I rang up to check on the roads,' Jack told her, making the fire safe. 'Apparently there's a lot of surface water in places, so I'll drive you back in the Jeep. I'll have your car sent to Park Crescent in the morning.'

Kate eyed him militantly. This was the last thing she wanted. 'I'm perfectly capable of driving through a few puddles.'

'The river's broken its banks at one place. Your car is too small to cope,' he said in a tone that warned her not to argue.

'I don't want to put you out—'

'You're not. I was driving into town to see Dad, anyway. If you'll get your things I'll bring the Jeep round.'

Feeling well and truly put in her place, Kate went up to the guest room. She removed the sweatshirt, folded it neatly and left it on the bed, put on her camisole and suit jacket and went downstairs. Jack was waiting with her raincoat over his arm. He held it out, and in silence Kate put it on and belted it tightly.

'I'll just say goodbye to Bran before I go.'

'No need. He's coming with us.'

The sunshine had gone, leaving an overcast afternoon as dark as Kate's mood as Jack helped her up into the Jeep, her only consolation the welcome from Bran behind his wire screen.

When they reached the main road there were large stretches of surface water in some places. As they drew nearer the river, the water grew deeper and Kate realised that Jack had been right. Only a four wheel drive could have made the journey in safety.

'If you can't get my car back tomorrow it doesn't matter,' she told Jack. 'I can walk into town if I need anything.'

'Fine.'

And that was the sum total of their conversation until they arrived in Park Crescent. Instead of getting out right away, Jack looked at her for a long moment and she waited in foreboding, sure she wouldn't like what he had to say.

'I made a big mistake when I asked you to share my bed last night,' he said at last.

'And I made an even bigger one in agreeing.' Kate gave him a mirthless smile. 'I realise now that there was a much better solution to the sleepwalking problem. Instead of sharing your bed I should have taken Bran up to the guest room to share mine.'

'Dogs aren't allowed upstairs in Mill House,' Jack said after a pause, and got out. He came round to lift her down, and then waited while she unlocked her door and de-activated her alarm.

'Thank you for driving me home,' Kate said politely.

'My pleasure,' he said with sarcasm.

'Goodbye, Jack.' She closed the door, turned the key in the lock and rammed the bolts home hard enough for him to hear.

It was only after the Jeep moved off that she conceded that Jack had every right to be angry. Even hurt. This was the second time she'd rejected him.

As she went upstairs to change her clothes Kate felt a deep, mounting sense of guilt. For the first time in her life she had let her hormones take control. She had known, in her heart of hearts, that if she let Jack make love to her he would take it as a sign of something far more significant than mere sex. Last night, when he was smiling at her down the length of his dinner table, it was obvious that he'd taken it for granted they were back together again in every sense of the word. But she'd assumed he just wanted them to be lovers again. The idea of marriage had never occurred to her.

If only it hadn't rained so much.

Kate pulled on thick socks and jeans and a heavy sweater and tied her hair back from her tired face. She eyed her reflection with distaste. The way she looked now it was pretty amazing that Jack had wanted her at all. But their relationship had never been about looks. It was about the kind of rapport they'd shared over lunch today as much as the heat and rapture of their lovemaking earlier on. And there was no use blaming the rain. Without the flooding she wouldn't have stayed the night, it was true. But even after the upset about the sleepwalking she should still have had the strength to control her own libido in broad daylight. She scowled at herself. Normally she never noticed that she had a libido. With Jack it was different. Just one look from those silver-flecked grey eyes and every clamouring hormone she possessed ran riot.

CHAPTER TEN

THAT weekend marked a downward turn in Kate's 'tidy little life'. Her painting and decorating was finished, it was too cold to start gardening, and it was so hard to fill her free time she accepted another client. When she found her keys posted through the door and her car parked outside she wrote a polite letter of thanks to Jack, but after that had no further contact with him of any kind. And felt the lack of his forceful presence in her life just as painfully second time round as the first.

Over supper mid week Anna was agog to hear details of the sleepover at Mill House. Armed against this in advance, Kate reported that she'd slept in a guest bed and stayed for lunch next day, after which Jack had driven her home in the Jeep.

Anna sighed, disappointed. 'We thought there might have been more to it than that.'

'You did, not me,' protested Ben. 'Leave the girl alone.'

Kate blew him a kiss. 'Thanks for the "girl" bit.'

'Pity though,' said Anna with regret. 'I hoped that spending the night together would do the trick.'

'We didn't spend the night together,' Kate reminded her. At least, not all of it.

Kate was heartily glad when the weekend arrived at last and she could make for Manor House School to spend a few happy hours with Joanna. The time with her passed far too quickly, as always, and Kate was in melancholy mood after taking Jo back to school that evening. When Philip Brace intercepted her in the car park she was pleased to see him and this time, with nothing in the world to hurry home for, she accepted his offer of a drink or coffee in the nearest pub before the drive back. Philip was an interesting companion and the interlude was pleasant, but when he saw her to her car afterwards Kate thanked him rather formally for the coffee and his company.

'No doubt we'll see each other at school again some time.'

'I'll look forward to it,' he assured her, his wry smile telling her he knew exactly where she was coming from.

Kate's mood deteriorated on the journey home. There was no point in encouraging Philip Brace—or anyone else. The only man she wanted in her life was Jack Logan. And fat chance there was of that that now. She would just have to make the best of life without him. Again. Easy to decide, she thought morosely, but hard to put into practice, even though Jack could have been on another planet for all she knew until she met his father in the park one Saturday afternoon with Bran.

'What the devil happened between you two, Kate?' Tom Logan asked bluntly when the greetings were over.

Kate fondled the dog instead of meeting his eyes. 'What do you mean?'

'You know perfectly well, my girl. Jack is like a bear with a sore head these days. When I see him, that is. He's either working all the hours that God sends on several projects at once, or driving to London—sometimes there and back the same day.'

And Kate, stabbed by jealousy, could well imagine why. 'I haven't seen him, Tom.'

'Which accounts for his permanent black mood!' He sighed. 'I was so sure you two would get back together. What went wrong, Kate?'

Kate smiled into the striking Logan eyes. 'How about I tell you over coffee at my place? You never did bring Bran to visit me.'

While Bran explored the garden Kate showed her visitor

over her house, anxious for his opinion. 'What do you think of it?'

'You've done a very good job,' he assured her. 'Your aunt would be pleased. The house would sell like the proverbial hot cake if you put it on the market.'

Kate shook her head. 'Not for sale. It's mine.'

'Just like Jack and that great house of his.' Tom followed her into the kitchen to call Bran inside and sat down at the table with the dog at his feet while Kate made coffee. 'But I'll say the same to you as I said to him; bricks and mortar are poor substitutes for a loving relationship.'

'True, but they cause a lot less pain.'

Tom nodded slowly. 'I grant you that.'

'You know Jack asked me to marry him?'

'Just the bare facts. He said you refused, but he wouldn't say another word.'

Kate heaved a sigh as she brought the tray over to the table. 'I hoped we could stay friends but Jack isn't having any.'

Tom looked her in the eye. 'This is the second time you've turned Jack down, remember.'

'I know.' She looked at him in appeal. 'I hope it doesn't change things between you and me.'

'Not in the slightest, love.'

To prove it, Tom Logan stayed with Kate until Bran grew restless. 'I'd better take this chap home. Shall I give Jack a message?'

Kate shook her head sadly. 'I doubt that he'd want one.'

Later that afternoon she thought for a brief, hopeful minute or two that she was wrong when a familiar florist's van drew up outside her house. Her spirits soared when she was given a basket of spring flowers but took an instant nosedive when she read the card. The flowers were from Richard Forster. Not Jack.

'Kate, your strategy worked like a charm. With heartfelt thanks, RF.'

Too bad she couldn't think of a strategy to improve her own life, she thought grimly.

A few days later Kate drove to collect Joanna for the Easter vacation.

'I'm dying to get out of my uniform,' said Jo, as they left the school car park. 'Are we having lunch on the way?'

'Would I expect you to survive if we didn't?' Kate teased. 'But not the posh hotel today; you can make do with a burger somewhere.'

'Cool! We don't get burgers in school.'

'At those fees I should hope not.' Kate glanced sideways to see a worried frown on Jo's face. 'What's up?'

The dark eyes gazed at her anxiously. 'I know it's terribly expensive to keep me there. Can you really afford it?'

'I don't have to, love. When you were a baby Robert took out an education insurance which covered your fees right up until you leave the place.' Kate patted her hand. 'There may be a few extras along the way due to cost of living and school trips and so on, but I can cope with that.'

'Can't you take the extras out of my money?'

'If it was absolutely necessary I could, but it's not, so chill, OK?'

Joanna Sutton was at the stage where she was an adult one minute and a child the next, but the child predominated as she raced through the rooms in Park Crescent, exclaiming in delight as she went.

'My room looks great! And I love the sitting room now it's furnished. Is that the paint colour I picked?'

'It certainly is. Your Coral Porcelain turned out well.'

Jo gazed round the room in approval, then turned a determined glance on Kate. 'I've got something to say.' She paused and took a deep breath. 'The thing is, I should have said it ages ago.'

'Spit it out, then,' said Kate in alarm. 'What's wrong?'

'Nothing. I just want to say thank you,' blurted Jo. 'For taking me on, I mean.'

'Oh, Joanna! No thanks necessary,' Kate assured her, weak with relief. 'I'm only too happy to "take you on".'

'You really mean that? I've been worried. You know, because you gave up your job and sold your flat and—'

'Hey! Let's get something straight here. I was about to resign from my job anyway. And I sold the flat because I inherited this house.'

'But you only came to live in it because I didn't want to stay in London after Mum and Dad died,' Jo reminded her.

'True,' Kate agreed and smiled into the anxious elfin face. 'But it was no sacrifice. I love the house and, though I'm sorry for the tragic circumstances that made it necessary, it's a great big bonus to have you sharing it with me. OK?'

'OK.' Joanna heaved a heartfelt sigh of relief.

'Right. Now you've got that off your chest ring Grandma and tell her you're home.'

Jo made her call, and reported that her grandparents were looking forward to her visit. 'I'll try not to wear them out,' she added, grinning.

'Good. We're having supper with Anna and Ben tonight, by the way.'

Jo beamed. 'Great! Is Anna OK?'

'Blooming. She's dying to see you. Pop upstairs for a bath while I unpack for you.'

'I'm supposed to do it myself,' Jo said, pulling a face.

Kate tapped her nose. 'I won't tell if you won't! Now go.'

A minute later there was a scream of delight from upstairs and Jo came hurtling into the kitchen in her briefs and the unnecessary minuscule bra she'd asked for because all her friends had one.

'The cropped jeans and stripy top in the wardrobe,' she panted, 'I just love them, Kate—thanks. Can I wear them tonight?'

'That was my plan. Now scoot.'

Jo tore back upstairs and returned later, the gleaming hair brushed, her slender, long-legged body graceful in denims and pink and lavender top. 'Well?' she demanded, doing a twirl. 'Do I look cool or what?'

Kate blinked at the transformation from schoolgirl into something else entirely. 'I don't know about cool, but you certainly look grown up,' she said with misgiving.

Jo punched the air in delight, then stopped, the joy suddenly draining from her face.

'What now?'

'I forgot for a minute,' she whispered guiltily.

'And so you should,' said Kate with emphasis. 'Your mother and father would want that.'

'I hope so. Because I'm much better lately. I hardly cry at all. Do you?'

Kate shook her head. 'Elizabeth disapproved of tears.'

'I know! When I fell down when I was little she used to dust me off and tell me to stop making a fuss.' Jo's mouth drooped. 'But I wouldn't like her to think I didn't grieve for her—and for Daddy.'

'Darling, you'll never forget them, and you're bound to miss both of them terribly at times, but they would want you to stop grieving now and get on with your life.' Kate took her hand. 'They made me your official guardian, remember, so you know they trusted me to take care of you. And I will.'

'I know that, Kate.' Jo smiled valiantly. 'What time are we due at Anna's?'

Joanna slept late next morning, and Kate, awake early as she always seemed to be lately, got up quietly and had finished her morning's work before Jo appeared in the study doorway, yawning widely.

'Sorry I slept so long, Kate.'

'Did you enjoy your lie in?'

Jo nodded with enthusiasm, pushing the hair out of her eyes. 'But if you want me to get up earlier I will. Mum would never let me stay in bed after nine.'

Kate switched off her computer and got up. 'Let's have some brunch.'

'The thing is, Jo,' she said, when they were tucking into bacon and eggs, 'in my opinion you get enough rules and regulations in school. That doesn't mean you've got *carte blanche* to run wild at home now you've only got me to answer to, but you're definitely entitled to a lie in on your first morning.'

'Thanks, Kate. I had such a great time with Anna and Ben, but I was really tired by the time we came home,' said Jo. 'But you didn't have a long sleep, and you've been working all morning.'

'Which means we can now go out to play,' said Kate promptly. 'Anna is meeting us at two to go shopping.'

'I enjoyed that enormously,' said Anna later, while they were waiting for tea and cakes in her favourite coffee shop. 'I adore spending other people's money.'

'You spent some of your own, too,' Kate reminded her.

'Anna just had to buy the baby something,' said Jo, and smiled in satisfaction. 'We did, too.'

'Hard to resist,' agreed Kate. 'If I were any sort of god-mother-to-be I'd be knitting those cute little white things instead of buying them, but I know my limitations.'

Anna chuckled. 'You're off the hook—both grandmothers are knitting furiously as we speak. Oops, I almost forgot.' She fished an envelope out of her handbag and handed it to Joanna. 'This is for you.'

Jo's eyes lit up like lamps when she took out a party invitation. 'Josh and Leo's birthday—it's a disco!' she added in excitement. 'I can wear some of my new stuff. What do you think—denim mini-skirt or white jeans?'

'Jeans!' said Kate and Anna in unison.

'The Careys are transforming their barn into a nightclub for the party, brave souls that they are,' said Anna. 'Ben's volunteered his services as extra doorman, and you can spend the evening with me, Auntie.'

With Joanna at home, life was no longer flat for Kate. The days took on an agreeable pattern, with a walk in the park every day as soon as Kate switched off the computer, and some kind of outing in the afternoon. On the first Sunday Kate put a chicken in to roast before the usual walk with Joanna in the park, and waved, smiling, as she saw Tom Logan coming along the lake path towards them with Bran.

Kate made the introductions as they met up with him, eyeing Tom in alarm. At close quarters he looked pale and drawn, in such contrast to his usual health and vitality that she took his hand to feel his pulse surreptitiously as he kissed her cheek. But his smile was warm as he turned to Joanna.

'I'm very glad to meet you, my dear. This handsome fellow is Bran, my son's dog.'

'How do you do, Mr Logan?' said Jo, and bent towards the dog in yearning. 'Will he let me stroke him?'

'As much as you like, pet. He laps it up.' Tom turned to Kate. 'Joanna's with you for the Easter holiday?'

'Most of it. I'm driving her to Worcester to stay with her grandparents later this afternoon, but only for a couple of days. She's invited to a party on Saturday.'

'It's a disco,' Joanna informed him.

He smiled indulgently. 'I'm sure you'll have a really good time, sweetheart. Are you going along as chaperon, Kate?'

She laughed. 'And spoil the fun? No way; I'm just the

chauffeur. Come back and have some coffee with us, Tom. Or better still, stay and share our roast chicken.'

He shook his head, his eyes on Joanna as she yearned over the dog. 'That's very kind of you, but Jack's due back from London in time for supper and I'm chef.'

'Are you sure you won't come back and just rest for a moment first?' asked Kate in an undertone. 'You don't look at all well.'

'I overdid it on the golf course yesterday, that's all, love. If you like dogs, Joanna,' he added, 'I'll bring Bran to see you another time.'

'I could walk him in the park for you,' she offered eagerly.

'I may take you up on that.' He turned to Kate and, to her surprise, hugged her close again as he said goodbye.

'Come and see us soon and, in the meantime, go easy on the golf.' She kissed his cheek affectionately.

'Goodbye, Mr Logan.' Jo bent to stroke the wagging dog one last time. 'See you later, Bran.'

Kate sent Joanna upstairs to pack while she checked on the vegetables roasting in the oven with the chicken, and then stood gazing out of the window.

'What's the matter?' said Jo, returning with a holdall.

'I'm really quite worried about Mr Logan. He looked very unwell—and normally he's as fit as a fiddle.'

'I hope he's not ill. I liked him—and I just adored Bran.' Joanna sighed. 'I love dogs, but Mum didn't, so I couldn't have one.'

'Neither could I, same reason,' said Kate, and got up briskly. 'Right then, let's get this lunch on the table. And no seconds today,' she warned. 'Grandma will probably have an enormous tea waiting for you.'

The drive to Worcester through the afternoon sunshine was pleasant, and the Suttons so welcoming that Kate gave in to their urging and spent an hour with them before leaving. And was glad she had when she got home. Without Jo the house seemed deadly quiet. Kate rang her to report in then stretched out on the chaise with a book and the Sunday papers. And wondered how Jack had spent his weekend.

At that precise moment Jack Logan was on his way home from London in determined mood. He'd spent the previous evening with a woman who was attractive, intelligent and very good company when their various commitments allowed them to spend time together. Hester Morris was a high-flyer with a successful career in advertising, and outspoken about having no desire for marriage and children. He liked her very much, and enjoyed their no-strings relationship. But their first evening together since Kate's reappearance had been oddly unsatisfactory and, cursing himself for a fool, Jack had pleaded an oncoming migraine after dinner and rung for a taxi. Hester had taken it in her stride and Jack had kissed her cheek, promised to get in touch soon, and went back to his own bed to avoid sharing Hester's. He'd never had a migraine in his life, but on the spur of the moment it had been the only excuse he could think of to avoid hurting someone he valued as a friend.

As he turned off the motorway to make for home Jack looked truth in the face. Life with Kate for a friend was a hell of a sight more bearable than life without her. He'd call round tonight and tell her that, and hope to God she hadn't changed her mind since he saw her last. Her niece would be home for the Easter vacation by now, of course, but the little girl would surely be in bed if he left it late enough. He smiled sardonically. After forcing himself to keep away from Kate for weeks, his welcome was unlikely to be warm whatever time it was. After supper he would ask his father to keep Bran until tomorrow so he could stay with Kate long enough to make his peace—if she let him through the door.

Kate had just laid a tray with a chicken sandwich and a cup of coffee when the bell rang. Her heart took a flying leap against her ribs as she went into the hall. Jack Logan was the only man tall enough to identify through the fanlight over the front door. She clamped down on a rush of delight and smiled coolly as she opened the door.

'Why, hello, Jack. This is a surprise.'

'Let me in, please,' he said brusquely.

'Why?' she demanded, angered by his peremptory tone.

'I have something to show you.'

'You're interrupting my supper.'

'Are you alone?'

'Yes.'

'Good, because we need to talk. This is important, Kate.'

'It had better be. Close the door behind you.'

Jack followed her into the sitting room, eyeing the tray on the Pembroke table. 'One sandwich? Not much of a supper.'

'Big lunch.' Kate stood with arms folded. 'But you didn't come here to discuss my eating habits, so show me whatever you want to show me—'

'And get out,' he finished for her.

'I hope I wouldn't be as rude as that.' She looked up at him, wishing she felt as indifferent to him as she was trying to make out. He obviously hadn't had time for a haircut lately and, in a battered trench coat over a crew neck sweater and cords, Jack looked so much like the young man she'd once fallen in love with it was hard to maintain her distance. But something in his demeanour was deeply disquieting.

'I had dinner with Dad before I came here. He asked me to show you these.' He handed her an envelope. 'Look inside.'

Kate looked at him questioningly, but Jack's expression gave nothing away. She withdrew two photographs from the envelope and sat down with a bump, feeling the colour drain from her face. Both studies were of the same girl, the first at Joanna's age, the second as a radiant, smiling bride in her twenties.

Jack tossed his raincoat on a chair and put a hand on her shoulder. 'Kate, are you all right?'

'No, I'm not all right,' she snapped, her eyes glued to the photographs. The girl in them had dark, curling hair, but otherwise the likeness to Joanna was unmistakeable. 'Who is this?' Though there was only one woman it could be.

'My mother. My father met her when the first photograph was taken. They were in school together.' Jack breathed in deeply. 'He thought he was seeing things when he met Joanna in the park this morning.'

Kate nodded slowly, her eyes on the photographs shaking in her unsteady hand. 'So that's why he looked so ill.'

'He idolised my mother. We both did.' Jack's deep, authoritative voice grew husky. 'You know she died when I was fifteen. It took me years to get over losing her. But Dad never has. Coming face to face with Joanna today was a hell of a shock to him.' He sat on the end of the chaise and put an ungentle finger under Kate's chin to tilt her face up to his. 'When were you going to tell me that we had a daughter?'

CHAPTER ELEVEN

'I WASN'T going to—ever.' Kate pushed his hand away and looked up at him with hostility. 'Because in the eyes of the world she's not our daughter, she's my *niece*, Jack. All the time she was growing up I had to stand back and look on from the sidelines while my child called someone else Mummy.'

His fists clenched. 'Why in God's name didn't you tell me you were pregnant?' he demanded, glaring at her.

She glared back in hot resentment. 'I didn't realise I was for a while! There was a lot going on in my life at the time: the move to London, getting to grips with the new job, living alone in digs.' She wrenched her eyes away. 'And pining for you, Jack.'

Kate had put her sickness and weariness down to the changes in her life at first, but eventually she bought a test kit that confirmed her fears. At the time the Suttons had been packing up, ready for the move to London. Kate went home that weekend, officially to give them a helping hand, in reality desperate to contact Jack and tell him about the baby. But Elizabeth met her at the bus station with the shattering news that Jack Logan had married Dawn Taylor the previous weekend, and Kate's life fell apart.

'Dear God!' Jack seized her hand again. 'If I'd known in time I would have paid Dawn off and married you right away, Kate.'

She snatched her hand away. 'Not the ideal way to start a marriage, Jack.'

'Better than letting you go it alone!'

She gave a mirthless little laugh. 'Ah, but I didn't go it

alone. Far from it. Liz guessed my little secret right away and seized her chance to acquire the child she couldn't have herself because, she informed me, she'd had to look after me instead of having a child of her own. This was payback time.'

Jack sat back, his face haggard. 'No wonder she slammed the door in my face when I came looking for you. She was afraid to let me see the baby.'

Elizabeth's plans were cut and dried before Kate returned to London that terrible weekend. The Suttons would bring Kate's baby up as their own on condition that she obeyed their rules.

Jack looked sick. 'Don't tell me they sent you off to some kind of home!'

Kate shook her head. 'Nothing so dramatic. Elizabeth merely insisted I live with them in the new house in London. She wanted to make sure I took vitamins and received regular medical attention so that ''her'' baby would be a perfect, healthy specimen. She had no qualms about the father. She went off you big time when you married someone else, of course, but from a breeding point of view the Logan genes were perfectly acceptable.'

'I'm so glad my pedigree came up to scratch,' said Jack savagely. 'Did you manage to keep working?'

'Yes, thank God.'

Kate had always been slender. And, because morning sickness and misery over her situation killed her appetite, her shape altered so little her condition went unnoticed at work. She was passionately grateful for it. Her job was the only thing that kept her sane. She worked well into her sixth month, and by buying clothes a size or two larger than usual managed to disguise her not very considerable weight gain and keep her secret.

'I managed to carry on keeping my secret,' Kate told Jack, 'because at that stage I developed a kidney infection and had to take time off. I also suffered from depression, and sank into such depths of hormonal despair Liz and Robert decided to move to another part of London where no one knew us.'

Jack frowned. 'Surely neighbours must have noticed you were pregnant?'

'I never met Elizabeth's neighbours. Or wanted to. Besides, I was ill for quite a while, and even when I got better I never went out except to the antenatal clinic and for a daily walk in some park Liz drove me to, as far from home as possible. I felt like the skeleton in the closet!' Kate smiled grimly. 'It was around then that the sleepwalking started. Eventually Liz was so afraid I'd fall and harm the baby that Robert put a bed in the dining room on the ground floor, and I slept there until Jo was born.'

Jack closed his eyes for a moment. 'God, what a life! You must have hated my guts.'

She shook her head. 'No, Jack, I missed you and grieved for you, but I didn't hate you. After all, I was the one who left you and opted for a clean break. I could hardly object when you found someone else. Anyway the sleepwalking phase didn't last long because I went into labour a month early.' Kate looked away. 'I had a Caesarean section, which is why I wouldn't let you undress me that day. I didn't want you to see my scar.'

Jack grasped her hand so tightly she protested, and he lifted it to his lips in apology. 'Go on, darling. Tell me the rest.'

Kate faltered slightly at the endearment, but went doggedly on to talk about the deal with Liz, which meant handing the baby over the moment it was born. But when Kate went into labour both Suttons had such heavy colds they were barred from the maternity ward.

Kate sighed deeply. 'So I was the first to see her, and I loved her so much, Jack. I used to stand gazing at her for ages in the baby unit. She had to stay there for a while because she came early, and I had to go home without her. It was such a terrible wrench to leave her behind that I told Liz the deal was off. I wanted to keep my baby after all.'

'What changed your mind?' asked Jack with compassion.

'Liz was the only mother I ever knew, remember, and a pretty forceful personality. She played on the guilt angle that responsibility for me had kept her from having a child of her own, and this was a perfect way to repay the debt.'

Kate tried to sound dispassionate as she told Jack how her sister kept hammering on that to support a child Kate would have to work full-time and pay a child-minder. If she did that, Liz threatened to wash her hands of her. Kate would be forced to bring up her baby on her own in some poky bedsitter and farm her out to strangers so she could keep working. At that point post-natal depression hit Kate so hard she was in a terrible state by the time Joanna was discharged and Elizabeth took full advantage of it.

'I was in no condition to look after a child, physically, mentally or financially, she told me. She, on the other hand, could give my baby a good home, constant care and attention, and when the time came Robert would pay for a good school.' Kate took in a deep breath. 'In desperation I finally caved in, totally brainwashed about the good of my child, but I had to stick to Sutton rules. I was forbidden to give my baby her bottle, or bathe and change her, or even pick her up when she was crying in case she bonded to me and not Liz. But I dug my heels in and made two rules of my own. I insisted that I was made Jo's legal guardian, and that I chose her name. But I had no say in it when they sent her to boarding school at the age of eight,' Kate added bitterly.

Jack got up and paced round the room like a restless tiger. 'Did they keep you shut up in a downstairs room again after the baby was born?'

'No, of course not. But I went back to work far sooner than I should have because it was such torture to watch Liz do all the things I should have been doing for my baby girl. And, in the end, even though it broke my heart to leave her, I answered Anna's advertisement for a flat share.'

He frowned. 'Does Anna know about any of this?'

'No. I told her I was recovering from a broken engagement, which was no lie, Jack. And Anna finds it quite natural that I'm so attached to my "niece", because she is, too.'

He looked at her questioningly. 'What do I tell my father?'

'The truth, what else?'

Jack sat on the end of the chaise and took her hand again. 'Once Dad told me about meeting Joanna I realised why you won't marry me. But what I don't understand,' he added, 'is why you brought her here to live. You must have known I'd meet her one day.'

Kate shrugged. 'I thought it didn't matter if you did. I never saw a photograph of your mother, remember, and Jo doesn't resemble you or me in any way, except for my kind of body shape. I had no intention of turning up on your doorstep and confronting you with your love child, I assure you.' She looked down at their clasped hands. 'Personally, I wasn't keen on coming back here. Even after all these years I didn't relish the idea of seeing you play happy families with Dawn. But Joanna was desperate to get away from London after Liz and Robert died, and there was this house, just waiting for us to move into it. Jo fell in love with it, so here we are.'

Jack was silent for a while, then got up and stood over Kate, his eyes implacable. 'Right. This is what we do. Now I know the truth, you and I simply get married and—'

'Live happily ever after?' She shook her head. 'There's nothing simple about it. You're not thinking straight.'

He sat down again, his eyes boring into hers. 'One thing I do have straight. We *must* tell Joanna.'

Kate's eyes blazed. 'And just what are "we" going to tell her, Jack? That her Daddy married someone else the minute my back was turned, and I gave my baby away like a pound of tea because I couldn't face life as a single mother?

Something,' she added with bitterness, 'I've regretted every single day of my life since.'

'Then it's time to change things.' Jack's hand tightened on hers. 'Surely Joanna could cope with the facts if you explained them to her?'

She gazed at him in anguish. 'How can I do that to her, Jack? She's just lost the people she knew as parents. It would be like taking them away from her all over again.'

'She has two real live parents to take their place.'

'I can't take the risk.' Kate shivered. 'If I tell her the truth she might hate me. I won't do it, Jack.'

'Better than having her find out by accident.'

'I don't know. Maybe you're right. But Jo's so vulnerable right now.'

'Does she know anything about me?'

'Only that I've been seeing an old friend.'

He shrugged. 'Then she'll think it perfectly natural if you keep on seeing me.'

'So she can get used to having you around?'

'I want a whole lot more than that!' He touched a hand to her cheek. 'These past few weeks I've tried to prove to myself that I can live without you, Kate, but only proved that I can't. On the way home from London today, hours before I knew the truth about Joanna, I decided to play it your way, as your friend or anything you want. But you know damn well that *I* want to be husband—and your friend. The two are not mutually exclusive. For God's sake, Kate, I love you. And, in spite of my past sins, I know you still love me.' He pulled her up out of her chair and held her by the shoulders. 'Are you going to tell me I'm wrong?'

She stared up into the compelling eyes for a long moment, then shook her head wearily. 'No. You're not wrong, Jack.' She leaned into him, her cheek against the soft wool of his sweater. 'But Joanna comes first.'

'Then I'll do my best to make her like me.'

'She likes your father.' Kate looked up at him with a wry little smile. 'And she fell madly in love with Bran.'

'Ah!' Jack's eyes gleamed. 'Does she know he's mine?'

'Yes.'

'Good. I'll use him as my trump card. When do I meet her?'

'I'm fetching her from Worcester on Tuesday, so come to supper on Wednesday, if you like. It would help pass the time for her until Saturday.'

'What's happening on Saturday?'

Kate told him about the disco and, to her amusement, Jack scowled in disapproval.

'You're letting her loose among teenage boys?'

'She's thirteen, Jack. And Ben will be on hand to help Jim Carey fend off gatecrashers, so she won't come to any harm.'

'I'll ring Jim and offer my help—'

'No, you will not, Jack! Get to know Joanna first before you start acting the heavy parent.'

He smiled reluctantly. 'All right. You win—this time.' He picked her up and sat down on the chaise with her on his lap. 'You do realise what this means?' he said, his eyes inches from hers.

'What does what mean?' she said unevenly.

'If you refuse to tell Joanna I'm her father I'll just have to marry her aunt and become her uncle.'

'No way. Living a lie isn't easy, Jack—I speak from experience.'

'I thought you'd say that,' he said with satisfaction. 'Then we revert to Plan A and get Joanna so used to having me around she'll probably start asking my intentions.'

'You haven't been around at all lately,' she reminded him tartly.

His eyes smouldered. 'Do you blame me? You turned me down for the second time, Kate.'

'Don't tell me you were heartbroken, Jack Logan,' she retorted. 'I happen to know you went back to your haunts in London!'

'Yes. For all the good it did me.' He held her closer, smiling ruefully as he told her about the unsuccessful evening with Hester Morris. 'You can laugh if you like.'

She shook her head, secretly so delighted she wanted to hug him until his ribs cracked. 'I didn't *want* to turn you down, Jack. You can see, now, why I did. Besides, I didn't turn you down flat the first time either. I just wanted to work in London for a while before getting married.' Kate sighed. 'I took it for granted I'd see you every weekend once you realised you couldn't live without me.'

'Which is exactly what happened,' he said grimly. 'Only fate—in the shape of Dawn—intervened.'

'And what a shape it was,' Kate retorted. 'No wonder you couldn't resist.'

Jack kissed her suddenly, holding her still when she tried to protest, and after a moment or two Kate gave up protesting and kissed him back. He raised his head, his eyes gleaming as he smoothed a lock of hair back from her face. 'It was nothing to do with her shape,' he said huskily. 'I was like a kid wanting comfort, and Dawn provided it as bait to hook a husband. Not that I'm blaming her—it was my mistake.'

'You paid through the nose for it, Jack!'

'You paid a far higher price than me. But we can't go on paying, Kate.' He kissed her again, his hands sliding into her hair to hold her still. She leaned into him and he smoothed a hand down her face, his forehead against hers. 'I want you so much,' he said hoarsely, and she clutched him closer, aroused by the note of desperation in his voice.

'Have you left Bran outside in the car?'

'No.' He put her away from him to look into her face. 'He's staying with Dad again tonight. Why?'

'I just wondered.' Kate relaxed against him again. 'I'm so

glad you know everything, Jack. It's been desperately hard to keep the truth from you.'

'You've never told anyone else? Not even the banker you were engaged to?'

'Not even David. While Elizabeth and Robert were alive I couldn't tell anyone.' She paused. 'Besides, you're the only one I ever wanted to tell, Jack.' And right now she also wanted him to pick her up and carry her upstairs to bed. She was trying to find a way to tell him that when Jack set her on her feet and stood up.

'I should be going. You look tired, Katie.'

She pulled a face. 'You mean I look like a hag.'

Jack smiled. 'You look so much the opposite of a hag I'd better go before I do something you'll regret.'

Kate looked him in the eye. 'Do you want to stay the night?' she said baldly.

With a groan of pure relief Jack picked her up and sat down with her on the chaise. 'Of course I want to stay the night!' he said roughly and rubbed his cheek against hers. 'Not just to make love, though God knows I want that so much I ache for you, Katie. But I need to hold you in my arms all night most of all, to make up for all those other nights when you weren't there.'

'My thoughts exactly.' She grinned as Jack stood up with her and set her on her feet. 'Only my version had you carrying me up to bed. But don't try it. The stairs here are too narrow.'

'No romance in getting you black and blue,' he agreed. 'You go up first so I can enjoy your back view.' He gave her a tap on the bottom and Kate gave him a smile of such radiance his eyes blazed in response.

'I've missed you, Jack.'

'I've missed you too.'

'Then why did you keep away?'

He smiled crookedly. 'Because I'm a stubborn idiot. I had to prove that I could, I suppose. But I'm here now.'

'Only because you wanted to show me your mother's photographs,' she reminded him as she started up the stairs.

'I had other reasons.' He followed her up so closely she could feel his breath on her neck. 'Some of them very pressing,' he added huskily as he picked her up on the landing. 'Even shorter journey this time,' he said with satisfaction, and carried her into the bedroom. 'In college a girl told me that carrying a woman to bed was the best foreplay of the lot.'

'So that's why you do it!' Kate chuckled as he sat down with her on the bed, holding her on his lap. 'And did it work with the lady in question?'

Jack shook his head regretfully. 'I never tried it. She was a gorgeous Amazon, built on generous lines. Think of the damage to my ego—and other parts—if I'd dropped her half-way!'

Kate let out a snort of laughter as she hugged him close. 'She was right, though. It does appeal to the female in a woman.'

'It helps when the female is a featherweight. Like you.'

'You mean skinny,' she said, resigned.

He undid the buttons on her shirt and peeled it off, then turned her away from him to unclasp her bra. 'Definitely not skinny—just fine, delicate bones covered with silky skin,' he said unevenly, and kissed the back of her neck as he caressed her breasts, taking deep satisfaction in her hurried breathing. Kate endured the exquisite torture for a moment, then twisted round and flung her arms round his neck and, with a relishing sound, he kissed her fiercely. Her hands slid under his sweater, tugging at it until he yanked it over his head and pulled her against his chest.

'Wait,' said Kate hoarsely, and stood up to kick off her suede boots and undo the zip of the tailored trousers she'd worn for the trip to Worcester. Holding his eyes, she slid them off, removing the strip of lace beneath at the same time, and Jack went down on his knees to kiss her scar. She stood as still as she could under the gentle caress, but the hurried frantic rhythm of her breathing gave her away as his lips moved lower and lower until his tongue penetrated moist heat to find the tiny secret part of her that quivered, erect in its hiding place, so exquisitely sensitive that when his caresses homed in on it she gasped and stiffened, her hands fisted in his hair as waves of sensation swept over her.

Jack got to his feet and laid her on the bed, looking down at her in such triumphant possession Kate felt a throb of fiery response in the place where he'd just caused such havoc. He stripped off the rest of his clothes and joined her, uttering a visceral groan of pure pleasure as their bodies came into full naked contact.

'Firstly, I've now seen—and kissed—the famous scar,' he said against her mouth.

'Not only the scar!' She thrust herself closer, her eyes gleaming in triumph as she felt his erection nudge against her.

'Secondly, and maybe thirdly and fourthly, I want to do this—and this.' He slid his hands down her spine, then up to her breasts, cupping them as he bent his head to take a nipple into his mouth, his fingers teasing its twin. She made a sound he stifled with a kiss, and then moved his lips over her face as his hands continued such subtle torment she felt she'd die if he didn't take her soon and, just as she was about to pummel him in desperate demand, he sheathed himself inside her to the hilt and she gave a moan of passionate relief.

'I love you so much, Katie,' he said, his voice gruff with the raw need he was fighting to keep in check.

'I love you, too,' she said breathlessly, the last word swallowed in a gasp as he began to move and her body responded ardently as he thrust harder and deeper. Her hips rose to meet him, flesh meeting flesh as the relentless rhythm accelerated to a wild crescendo that sent her gasping into orbit seconds before his own release engulfed him and she held his face to her breasts in fierce possession as his body poured its tribute into hers before collapsing on top of her, taking away what little breath she had left.

When he found the will to move, Jack turned over on his back, rolling her with him and Kate drew in a deep, reviving breath as she settled in the crook of his arm.

'This is how it should have been all along,' he said, a lazy note of contentment in his voice.

'If we had been together all along—fourteen years to be precise—we would be an old married couple, and "this" as you put it, would surely be less frenetic by now,' Kate pointed out.

'I meant just being here together, in bed in each other's arms instead of all the nights we spent alone. At least I did,' he added, and put her away a fraction to look into her eyes. 'You shared a bed with this banker of yours.'

'You make that sound like a rude word,' she protested. 'His name was David, and I was engaged to him. Of course we shared a bed. But he had a television in the bedroom so I often fell asleep while he was watching England play cricket on the other side of the world, or whatever.'

'No wonder you packed him in.' He pulled her closer, his cheek against hers. 'When you come to live at Mill House you sleep—or not sleep—with me. No television in my bedroom.'

'I noticed,' she said absently, and pulled back a little, frowning. 'Jack, if we manage to sort things out with Joanna, and we do move in with you at Mill House one day, what will I do with this one? I hate the thought of selling it.'

'Make it over to Joanna,' he said promptly. 'It can be leased out until she's old enough to decide what happens to it.'

Kate sighed. 'It sounds so easy when you talk about it like that, Jack, but first we've got to get over this great big hurdle of telling her she's ours.'

'At least you said "ours" not "mine",' he said, kissing her.

Kate kissed him back, then turned to look at her alarm

clock. 'It's after midnight,' she said with regret. 'Time you were going, Jack.'

He pulled her close again. 'Why?'

'You work long hours and need your sleep. Besides,' she added, batting her eyelashes at him, 'I'm not sure I want that Jensen of yours parked outside my house all night.'

'I came in the Jeep.' Jack smiled triumphantly. 'And I left it near the park gates, well away from your smart front door.'

'Did you now!' Kate's eyes narrowed speculatively. '*And* you left Bran with your father.'

'I certainly did.'

'So you intended to stay from the start.'

'While I was driving from London I decided to come here after seeing Dad and tell you I was ready to do any damn thing you wanted as long as we were part of each other's lives again. I left Bran with him so I could spend time persuading you after Jo was in bed.' He smiled crookedly. 'I thought she was much younger than she actually is, Kate. When Dad mentioned the photographs the truth hit me in the face.'

Kate looked at him in entreaty. 'Were you angry with me, Jack?'

'I was euphoric!' He pulled her close, his cheek against hers. 'I'm still trying to come to terms with the miraculous fact that we've got a daughter. All I have to do now is persuade you to let her know she's got a real live father—and a mother I want to marry as soon as I can get the ring on her finger.'

Kate stirred next morning, afraid she was dreaming again when she felt the touch of coaxing lips and hands. But she opened her eyes to find Jack was there in the flesh, real and warm and already aroused as he caressed her awake. He kissed her in tender possession as he slid slowly home inside her, waking all her senses one by one, the subtle seduction so perfect she never wanted it to end and held him close to experience every last nuance of pleasure as the throbbing died away.

'Good morning,' he said against her mouth.

'It certainly is,' she agreed breathlessly and winced as she looked at the clock. 'A very early good morning, Jack!'

'Some people go out to work,' he told her and slid from the bed to pull on his clothes. 'And, much as I'd like to stay all day with you in that bed, I must dash home to shower and dress. I'll scribble a note to Molly to leave us something for dinner, and pick you up tonight about seven. Unless,' he added, looking down at her, 'you have something better to do?'

'I haven't got my diary with me, but offhand I can't think of anything,' she said flippantly, then smiled at him. 'What could possibly be better?'

'Exactly. What are you going to do after I've gone?'

'My usual shift at the computer.' She looked at him questioningly. 'I thought I'd ask your father round to lunch later and tell him my story. Or would you rather do that yourself?'

Jack leaned over to kiss her. 'No, my darling. You tell him—it's your story.

'It's yours too!'

'But you're the heroine; I'm just the villain of the piece.'

She shook her head. 'Not to me, Jack.'

He pulled her up into his arms. 'Then from now on I'll do my damnedest to be the hero.' He kissed her again and, with a deep sigh of regret, let her go. 'I'll see you later.'

Kate forged through her morning's work, then rang the Suttons in Worcester to talk to Joanna and, once assured that her child was well and happy, Kate rang Tom Logan and suggested he come round for a sandwich lunch.

When he arrived, looking rested and with his colour back, she threw her arms round him in relief. 'Thank goodness, you look yourself again! You had me really worried yesterday.'

'No wonder. When I saw Joanna I swear my heart stopped for a moment. I couldn't believe my eyes. She was my Margaret to the life!' Tom kissed her cheek. 'Jack rang earlier to check on me. He sounded happy, Kate.'

She smiled radiantly, then bit her lip. 'I'm happy too, except for one thing. I have to tell Joanna the truth, and I'm such a coward about it, Tom.' Kate led him into the kitchen and took the cover from a platter of chicken sandwiches. 'Help yourself; I'll eat and talk at the same time.'

She told her story again briefly and succinctly, editing out the parts that would cause him unnecessary pain.

'My dear girl,' he said, shaken. 'To think you've had to keep this to yourself all these years.' He reached across the table to take her hand. 'But now, my love, you've got to bite the bullet and tell Joanna.'

Kate nodded reluctantly. 'But not until after the party. I want her to enjoy that before I hit her with the truth.'

Tom Logan's grasp tightened. 'In my opinion you and Jack should tell her together.'

'She needn't hear about Dawn and the baby. I'll tell her I broke up with Jack—which is true—and he married someone else on the rebound before I knew I was expecting his child.'

Tom shook his head. 'Even at first glance Joanna strikes me as mature for her age. I think she deserves the truth, warts and all. I'll make that clear to Jack when he comes to collect the dog.'

'I can't say I agree with Dad,' said Jack later, as Kate received a warm welcome from Bran in the Jeep. 'I haven't even met her yet, but I don't relish telling my daughter I was such a fool over Dawn.'

'Then don't,' said Kate firmly. 'We'll play it my way, and give Jo the abridged version.'

'Thank you, darling. I've never thought of myself as a coward until now. But then,' he added, 'I didn't know I was a father until now, either.'

When they got to Mill House they went for a walk in the gardens with the dog before dinner, arms around each other like teenagers as they circled the millpond. Afterwards Jack went up for a shower while Kate sat in front of the fire in the living room with Bran to wait for him, her eyes thoughtful as she gazed into the flames.

'What at you thinking about?' asked Jack, as he joined her.

'Would you mind if we told Joanna our story here?' Kate curled up against him. 'No matter how she takes it, she still has to live with me afterwards, so I'd rather we didn't have the showdown in Park Crescent.'

'You'd rather my house was ruined for her than yours,' said Jack ruefully.

She nodded. 'I tend to think in worst scenario terms.'

'In which you've had some experience,' he said grimly.

'So have you. But let's not spoil our evening by worrying about it. What did Molly leave us for dinner?'

By mutual consent there was no more talk of the coming confession. Instead Kate told Jack everything she could about his daughter as they enjoyed fillet of lamb cooked with garlic, thyme and cannelloni beans. They spent an hour in front of the fire afterwards and then took Bran out for a walk, but when they'd settled him down for the night Jack took Kate's hand and led her straight upstairs.

'I've got some lonely nights in front of me, so let's go to bed,' he said firmly, and she rubbed her face against his sleeve.

'Yes, please!'

Jack drove Kate home early the following morning and kissed her goodbye with tension she felt as keenly as he did.

'I'll leave you in peace with Joanna tonight,' he said, holding her tightly.

'Come to supper tomorrow, then,' said Kate.

'I've got a board meeting that day,' he said wryly. 'It's going to be hard to keep my mind on the job, when all I can think of is meeting my daughter for the first time.'

CHAPTER TWELVE

'IT WAS lovely to see Grandma and Grandpa,' said Joanna, on the journey from Worcester, 'but I'm glad to be going home. I missed you, Kate.'

'I missed you, too.'

'What did you do while I was away?'

'I worked, as usual, and I had dinner with Jack Logan—'

'The old friend with the great dog,' said Jo promptly, and slanted a cheeky grin at her. 'Did you have a nice time?'

'Very nice, thank you,' said Kate primly. 'I thought you might like to meet him too, so I asked him to supper tomorrow. We'll stop in town on the way home and buy some food.'

'Is he bringing Bran with him?'

'No. But if you play your cards right Jack might ask you round to his place to play with Bran in the garden there. It's huge, with a millpond.'

'Is he rich then?'

'He's well off, certainly, but only because he's worked very hard to achieve it.'

'Will I like him?'

'I don't know. I hope so, Jo, because I like him a lot.'

'Then I expect I will, too.'

'I'm glad we've got a guest for supper,' said Jo the next day, as she took a tray of cupcakes out of the oven. 'It takes my mind off the party.' She smiled sheepishly. 'I keep thinking about it all the time.'

Praying that the party would live up to her expectations,

Kate handed her the icing sugar. 'How are you going to dec-orate the cakes?'

Jo eyed them with satisfaction. 'I thought white icing with a chocolate mini Easter egg to finish them off. They came out well, didn't they? I hope Mr Logan likes cake.'

'He'll love those,' said Kate with absolute certainty. 'But I think you'd better call him Jack, to avoid confusion with his father.'

As seven-thirty approached Kate wondered if Jack was in an equal state of tension. To avoid formality they were eating in the kitchen and the dress code was jeans and sweaters. Blissfully unaware of the emotion almost choking Kate, Jo laid the small kitchen table with a checked cloth, put red can-dles on white saucers, and then went into the sitting room to set out nuts and savoury biscuits. Kate did some deep breathing exercises, checked on her tomato sauce, fiddled with her hair, put some lipstick on, then tensed at the sound of a car and went into the hall.

'That sounds like Jack's beloved Jensen,' she said, amazed that her voice sounded so normal.

'Shall I go?' asked Jo when the bell rang, and Kate nodded, rigid with stage fright as she watched Jo open the door to her tall father, who stood equally still as he set eyes on his daugh-ter for the first time.

'Hello,' he said at last, and smiled down into the dark eyes surveying him with frank interest. 'I'm Jack Logan.'

'Hi, I'm Joanna.' She smiled warmly. 'You look like your father—I met him on Sunday with your gorgeous dog.'

'Thank you, I'll take that as a big compliment. I hope you like these.' Jack handed her a brightly wrapped package, then held out an armful of pink and white lilies to Kate and kissed her very deliberately on the mouth. 'You look very beautiful tonight.'

'Thank you, these are lovely,' Kate said breathlessly, her

colour high. 'Go into the sitting room with Jo while I put these in water. What did you get, love?'

'Chocolates!' said Jo with relish and turned to Jack. 'Thank you—' She hesitated. 'Kate said I should call you Jack. Is that OK?'

'Absolutely,' he assured her and exchanged a look with Kate that spoke volumes.

'How about a beer?' she said huskily. 'Back in a moment.'

Kate put the lilies into a jug of water, poured beer into a glass and went back to the sitting room, relaxing slightly when she found Jo curled up in a chair, chatting easily with Jack about her stay with her grandparents.

'I forgot to tell you, Kate,' she said. 'When I had tea in a café in Worcester with Grandma I saw Leah Brace from school. She was with her father. He sent you his regards.'

'How nice of him.' Kate avoided Jack's eyes as she handed him his beer. 'Let's sit down. Supper's not quite ready yet.'

He took the foot of the chaise, smiling at Jo. 'Kate tells me you're going to a party on Saturday.'

She nodded, eyes sparkling. 'The Carey twins invited me. Do you know them?'

'I know their father.' He smiled wryly. 'I didn't realise Jim's twins were old enough for disco parties.'

'It's their fourteenth birthday,' Jo informed him. 'The party sounds like fun, it's in a barn.'

Kate sat with them for a while, content to sit in silence while the two people she loved best in the world got to know each other, but after a while she excused herself to see to the meal.

'Shall I help?' said Jo, jumping up.

'Stay and entertain our guest,' said Kate. 'Just kitchen supper tonight, Jack,' she told him. 'I shan't be long.'

He smiled at her then turned to his daughter as he accepted the nuts she offered him. 'Tell me about school, Joanna. What subjects do you like best?'

Finding it hard to tear herself away, Kate went back to the kitchen to grill bacon to crispness while water heated for the pasta. She put bowls in the oven to warm, set out dishes of grated cheese on the table, filled wineglasses and cut thick slices from a loaf of Italian bread, checked on her sauce, plunged the pasta into the pot and went to fetch the others.

Joanna talked with complete ease as she helped serve the meal, laughing when Jack told her that the last time he'd had supper with Kate she hadn't honoured him with her culinary skill.

'We sent out for Chinese,' he said, grinning at Kate. 'But this is much better. Great sauce.'

'We had great roast chicken on Sunday too, with herb stuffing and bread sauce,' Jo informed him. 'Kate's a good cook. But I expect you know that,' she added, twirling pasta round her fork.

'We hadn't seen each other for years until recently,' Jack said regretfully, 'so I'm not as familiar with her cooking skills as you, Jo. But I hope to be in future,' he added, his eyes spearing Kate's.

Jack insisted on helping to clear the table after the first course, which resulted in much bumping into each other as the three of them got in each other's way in the small kitchen.

'For heaven's sake, sit down, Jack,' laughed Kate at last. 'Leave the rest to us.' She shot him a meaningful glance as Jo put her cupcakes on the table.

'Those look good,' he said promptly. 'Did you make them yourself, Kate?'

She shook her head. 'Jo's work, not mine.'

'I won't mind if you don't like cake,' Jo assured him shyly. 'Kate's got some cheese.'

Jack took a cake, pronouncing it so delicious he asked for another. 'Best I've tasted in a long time,' he told her, and Joanna flushed with pleasure as she ate hers.

'Thank you. I like baking.'

'Just as well,' said Kate dryly. 'My culinary skills don't extend that far.'

They stayed at the table to drink coffee, Jo completely at ease with her new acquaintance as she asked questions about Bran.

'Come round to my house at the weekend to see him,' said Jack casually. 'I'll get Molly to organise a special Easter Sunday lunch.'

'Who's Molly?'

'She's the good fairy who cleans my house and leaves me delicious meals.'

'She's very young to be such a fabulous cook,' said Kate. 'I've sampled some of her food, Jo. It's delicious.'

'No more delicious than the meal I had tonight,' said Jack emphatically. 'So is that a date, Jo? Or will you be too tired after your party?'

She shook her head, smiling. 'I'd love to come.'

'I'll expect you about twelve, then. We can have a stroll with Bran in the garden before lunch.'

'Great,' said Jo, and got up. 'Past my bedtime,' she announced and leaned down to kiss Kate's cheek.

'Goodnight, darling, sleep well.'

Jo smiled as Jack got to his feet. 'It was nice to meet you. Thank you again for the chocolates. I'll look forward to Sunday.'

'So shall I,' he assured her.

Jo hesitated, then held up her face and Jack touched his lips to the smooth cheek, his voice husky as he bade his daughter goodnight.

When they were alone Kate exchanged a long look with Jack, then went into his arms with a shaky sigh.

'Well?' she said, tipping back her face. 'What do you think of our daughter?'

'She's a darling.' Jack leaned his forehead against hers. 'I can't believe she's ours. I hope to God we can tell her the truth without turning her against me.'

'And me,' she reminded him, but Jack shook his head.

'She very obviously thinks the world of you, so that won't happen, Kate. As I said before, I'm the villain of the piece.'

'We needn't tell her about Dawn—'

'But we will.' Jack raised his head. 'Meeting her tonight clarified that for me. If we have any hope of life together as a family, Jo must know everything.'

'I just wish we could tell her in a way that wouldn't hurt her—or you.' Kate took his hand. 'It's not late. Stay for a while, Jack. I need you.'

'I need you too,' he said with feeling, and drew her down on the chaise with him. 'Would our daughter be shocked if she saw me cuddling you?'

'She's thirteen, not three, Jack! She'd probably think it strange if we weren't.'

He laughed and rubbed his chin over her hair. 'Do you think she liked me?'

'Of course she did. Otherwise she wouldn't have been chatting away so happily.'

'I'll ask Dad round to lunch on Sunday, too. He can always take off later if he can't face the showdown.'

Kate nodded thoughtfully. 'Good idea. Jo liked him and, after all, he is her grandfather.'

'He knew that the moment he saw her, which is why he was knocked for six.' Jack sighed. 'I suppose I'd better be on my way. Shall I call in tomorrow?'

'Not tomorrow. Ben's away so we're sharing pizza and a video with Anna in the evening, but we're in on Friday. Come for a drink on your way home.'

'I'll finish early for once. I need to make the most of her while I can.' He stood up with Kate and set her on her feet. 'After Sunday's revelations she may never want to set eyes on me again.'

*   *   *

Jack's words stayed with Kate as she got ready for bed. It was hours before a dream-troubled sleep overtook her, but she woke early and got up feeling tired and heavy-eyed, in direct contrast to Joanna, who came bounding into the kitchen, full of the joys of spring.

'I like Jack,' she announced. 'He's easy to talk to, like Ben. Only better looking,' she added with a grin, and poured herself some orange juice. 'He's quite a hunk!'

'I'm glad you approve,' said Kate dryly. 'How about scrambled eggs?'

'No thanks. I'll just have yoghurt and toast.' Jo applied herself to her breakfast while Kate drank a cup of tea. 'Aren't you going to eat anything?'

'In a minute.'

'You look a bit pale.'

'I'll be fine after more tea.'

Joanna gave her a questioning look. 'When you knew him before, was Jack your boyfriend?'

'Yes.' Kate braced herself. 'In fact we were engaged briefly, but it didn't work out.'

'What happened?'

Kate busied herself with pouring tea. 'I was determined to work in London; Jack was equally determined to stay here, so we decided on a clean break.'

Jo frowned and reached for more toast. 'I bet you were both sorry afterwards.'

'Yes, we were.' Which was an understatement. Feeling like someone on the edge of a precipice, Kate changed the subject to Jo's choice of birthday present for the twins. 'We'd better pop into town this afternoon and find something.'

Jack rang before they went out, to ask if his daughter approved of him, and laughed, relieved, when Kate told him he was not only easy to talk to but better looking than Ben Maitland.

'You can't get higher praise than that,' Kate assured him.

'Thank God for it. I'll sleep a lot easier tonight than I did last night!'

'So what do you think of Kate's friend, Jo?' asked Anna that evening.

'I think he's lovely. Much better looking than David,' said Jo, startling Kate.

'You remember David, then?'

'Of course I do.' Jo pulled a face. 'He used to come to Sunday lunch sometimes when you were together. He talked down to me. You know, as if I was a baby—which I suppose I was then. But Ben and Jack treat me like an adult.'

'As they should,' said Anna, trying not to laugh. 'So you approve of Jack?'

Jo nodded, and flashed Kate an impudent smile. 'I think he wants to get back with you.'

'Do you, indeed!'

'Why do you think I went to bed so tactfully last night? I could tell he was dying to be alone with you.'

Kate stared at her, speechless, and Anna dissolved into helpless laughter.

'What do they teach you at that all girl establishment of yours?'

'It's a school, not a convent,' Jo pointed out. 'And some girls have boyfriends back home and bore you rigid about what they get up to with them. Not me, of course,' she said regretfully.

'Not yet,' murmured Anna, and helped Jo to more pizza. 'How would you feel if Jack Logan did get back with Auntie?' she asked bluntly, ignoring Kate's glare.

Jo thought about it as she munched. 'I wouldn't mind at all. He's cool. And he's potty about Kate.'

'Why do you think that?' demanded Kate, her colour high.

Jo gave her a pitying look. 'It was pretty obvious! Besides,' she said thoughtfully, 'you sort of look right together.'

When they got home Kate waited until Jo was in bed, then rang Jack to report on the topic of conversation over pizza at the Maitland house.

'Anna just asked her straight out?' said Jack, laughing. 'What did you do?'

'Blush,' said Kate succinctly. 'Trust Anna to ask the question I wouldn't dare to. Anyway, we're in the clear. She seems quite happy about you as the current man in my life.'

'The only man in your life! Was marriage mentioned?'

'Even Anna didn't go that far!'

'Pity. Jo's opinion would have been interesting.'

'She thinks we look sort of right together, if that's any comfort.'

'Damn right it is! Dad's very happy about Sunday, by the way. Last I heard he was off to buy the biggest Easter egg in town.'

'How sweet!' Kate took in a deep, unsteady breath. 'Oh, God, Jack, I do hope there's a happy ending to all this.'

'Amen to that. In the meantime I'll call in tomorrow evening to make the most of my daughter while I can.'

Jack's second visit was as much a success as the first. Joanna opened the door to him again and greeted him with such open pleasure that Kate could tell he wanted to hug her. He stayed for an hour, admired the sweatshirts purchased as birthday presents for the twins, and approved the white jeans and jade-green top Joanna fetched to show him.

'I was going to wear my mini-skirt to the party,' she told him, 'but Kate and Anna said the jeans would be better.'

'Try them on and show Jack how you'll look tomorrow, if you like,' said Kate, and Joanna rushed off immediately.

Jack groaned. 'Mini-skirt with those long legs?'

'My sentiments exactly,' said Kate, grinning. 'Anna's, too.'

Joanna came back into the room in her party gear, her eyes sparkling as she did a twirl. 'What do you think?' she asked Jack.

'Absolutely gorgeous,' he said without hesitation.

Kate and Joanna saw him to the door when he left soon afterwards, and Jack kissed Jo's cheek and Kate's mouth before getting into his car.

'You really like him, don't you?' said Jo as they waved him off.

'Yes, darling, I really do. Now, take the new things off and climb into your pyjamas. You need an early night tonight if you're partying tomorrow.'

It was hard to know who was the more tense when Kate delivered Joanna to the Carey house the following evening. Music was thumping from a barn decorated with fairy lights and a large streamer wishing Josh and Leo a happy birthday, and Jo took in a deep breath as the two boys raced towards her, their eyes snapping with excitement as she handed them the parcels she'd taken ages to pack earlier.

'Hi,' they said in unison as they tore away the paper. 'Great! Just what we wanted—thanks a lot.' They handed the presents to their mother and grabbed Jo's arm. 'Leave your coat with Mum and come *on*, it's party time!'

With anxious eyes Kate watched her ewe lamb run with the twins towards the lights and music, then turned to smile ruefully at their mother.

Megan Carey patted her hand. 'She'll have a great time. Don't worry; the others are a nice crowd of kids and Jim and Ben are on hand to keep a discreet eye on things.'

Kate thanked her warmly, told her she was at the Maitland house if needed and, with a last glance towards the barn, waved at Ben at his post on the door and went to join Anna.

As usual Anna's company was a calming influence as Kate reported on the previous evening.

'He seems to be calling in quite a lot lately. Are you still just good friends?'

'Jack wants more than that.'

'Of course he does—he's a man!' Anna looked at her curiously. 'Does he want to marry you?'

'Yes.'

'Do you want to marry *him*?'

'Yes.'

'Then what's stopping you—?' Anna breathed in sharply and put a hand on her stomach, her eyes wide.

Kate jumped to her feet in alarm. 'What's wrong?'

'Nothing at all.' A beatific smile spread over Anna's face. 'I think my baby just said hello for the first time.'

Kate hugged her. 'How lovely! Isn't it the most wonderful feeling—?' She bit her lip and stood back, colour rushing into her face as Anna stared at her in silent, wide-eyed question. Kate sat down abruptly and took in a deep breath. 'It's all going to come out tomorrow, anyway, so I'll tell you first, Anna. I remember exactly how it feels to be pregnant because, although she doesn't know it yet, Joanna is my daughter, not my niece.'

Anna gave a screech and pulled Kate into her arms, tears pouring down her face as she held her close for a long, emotional interval. 'Sorry, sorry!' she said at last. 'It's hormones. But you must know about that. For heaven's sake don't leave me in suspense, love—' She stopped dead and moved back to peer into Kate's face, swallowing hard. 'Oh, my God, it's Jack, isn't it? He's her father.'

Kate sat with her on the sofa and told her story with as little drama as possible, but by the end of it both of them were in tears again. 'So tomorrow, after Easter Sunday lunch at Mill House,' Kate finished thickly, 'Jack and I are going to make a clean breast of it and throw ourselves on our daughter's mercy. Funny, really,' she added, sniffing, 'I've kept my secret all these years, and now I've told my story three times in one week.'

'Three times?'

'Jack's father.'

'Oh, of *course*.' Anna blew out her cheeks. 'Poor man. He must have thought he was seeing a ghost if Jo looks that much like his wife.'

'She does. Margaret Logan had dark curling hair like Jack's, but otherwise it could have been Jo in the photograph. When I saw it the hairs stood up on the back of my neck.'

'I bet they did.' Anna let out a deep breath. 'It's a pity you're driving Jo home. You could do with a stiff drink. I know I could. But, since neither of us can indulge, let's have some coffee.'

In the end Kate made the coffee because Anna was in such a daze after the revelations that she couldn't concentrate enough to operate the machine. She was still talking about Jo when Kate's phone interrupted the flow.

'Joanna!' Kate spilt some coffee as she grabbed the phone, then blew out her cheeks in relief. 'Oh, Jack, thank God. I thought something was wrong with Jo.'

'Why?' he demanded. 'Didn't she want to go to the party?'

'She wanted to so much I just hope she isn't disappointed.'

'She won't be. She's probably having the time of her life. How did she look?'

'To quote you, Jack, she looked absolutely gorgeous.'

'In that case she's probably beating off dance partners with a stick. If they have dance partners these days. Tell her I want chapter and verse tomorrow.' Jack took in an audible breath. 'How the hell are we supposed to get any sleep tonight, Katie?'

'Beats me.' Kate glanced at her watch. 'Only half an hour to go and I pick her up.'

'Next time I'll do that—I hope.'

'I hope so too, Jack.'

'That was Daddy, worrying about his daughter, I assume,' said Anna, handing Kate a fresh cup of coffee.

'About tomorrow too, like me!'

'Try not to worry, love. Knowing Jo as I do, I'm sure she'll take it well.'

'I just keep thinking she'll hate me for giving her away.'

Anna put her arm round her. 'Jo loves you far too much to do that. She's also mature enough to understand why you felt you had to.'

When Kate arrived back at the Carey house the party had transferred to the kitchen where all the flushed, excited guests were consuming mugs of hot chocolate while they waited to be picked up. Jo was in the middle of an animated group in loud discussion over some pop band, totally unaware she was being watched, and Megan Carey laughed softly as she showed Kate into the room.

'Someone had a really great time, by the sound of it.'

Kate grinned. 'Not only Jo. Everyone else too.'

'Kate!' Jo's eyes lit up as she turned round.

'Hi. Did you have a good time?'

'The best,' said Jo simply, and with unaffected good manners thanked Megan and Jim Carey, then said her goodbyes to the group, who followed her outside to Kate's car to wave her off.

'Thanks again for the presents. See you Tuesday,' shouted Leo and Josh in unison.

Jo nodded vigorously and waved until the car reached a bend which took it out of sight of the house. 'That was such a cool party,' she told Kate with satisfaction. 'Great music, with a DJ, and there was a real bar. We had cocktails! Non-alcoholic,' she added hastily.

'I'm glad you enjoyed it, love,' said Kate with relief.

'Did you have a nice time with Anna? Silly question,' added Jo with a giggle. 'I expect you talked and drank coffee all night. Is she OK?'

'She's euphoric. She felt the baby move for the first time while I was there.'

'Wow!' said Jo, awed. 'Did she cry?'

'Yes, a bit,' admitted Kate. 'I even shed a godmotherly tear myself. Are you tired, darling?' she asked as they arrived home.

'I wasn't until now,' Jo admitted.

'Straight up to bed then. You need some sleep.'

'You do too, Kate; we're partying again tomorrow,' said Jo happily.

Kate woke up downstairs in the middle of the night, to find Joanna patting her hand.

'Oh, darling,' she said, shivering. 'I'm so sorry. Did I frighten you to death?'

'A bit. You came into my room, then sort of glided out again, so I got up to see if you were all right. You didn't answer me so I realised you were sleepwalking. A girl in my dorm does that.' Jo pulled a face. 'It's creepy, but Miss Hayes said sleepwalkers mustn't be shocked awake, so I followed you down here before I woke you. I'll get your dressing gown,' she added as Kate's teeth chattered. 'Then I'll make you some tea, or something.'

'You get the dressing gown, I'll make the tea,' said Kate. 'Sorry about this. It's a stupid habit.'

'I know. Mummy told me—shan't be long.' Joanna raced upstairs, and Kate pulled herself together and made for the kitchen to fill the kettle, glad to get into her dressing gown when Jo ran back with it.

'You should go back to bed,' she said sternly, holding it out.

Kate hugged her and promised that once she'd made their drinks she would do as she was told. Back in bed she drank her tea, then slid down under the covers, glad to get warm again while she waited for morning, knowing of old that she'd get no more sleep that night. But, to her delight, Jack rang before she got up.

'How are you, my darling?'

'All the better for hearing your voice, Jack,' she assured him.

'And how's our daughter? God, that gives me such a kick to say that. Did Jo enjoy the party?'

'She certainly did. I'll leave it to her to tell you the details.' Kate sighed. 'Time to get up, I suppose. What are you doing right now?'

'I'm in bed, waiting impatiently to see my two girls again.' His voice dropped a tone. 'I wish I had you here with me.'

Kate laughed, told him she loved him and ordered him to behave himself until she got to Mill House.

'Does that mean I don't have to once you come?'

'Certainly not,' she said primly. 'Thank you for ringing, Jack. I was feeling pretty tense.'

'I thought you might be. Do you feel better now?'

'Yes. I love you, Jack.'

She heard a quick intake of breath. 'I love you too, my darling. See you soon, and don't be late.'

Feeling a lot more prepared to face the day, Kate got up and had a bath, then came out to find Jo on the landing, her eyes anxious.

'Are you all right, Kate?'

'I'm fine. Sorry I gave you such a fright. I'd promise not to do it again, if I could.'

'I don't mind! I was just worried you might fall on the stairs.'

'It's never happened yet,' Kate assured her briskly. 'Right then, your turn in the bath.'

There was much discussion as to the appropriate wear for lunch at Mill House but knowing that Jo would inevitably spend time with Bran in the garden, Kate advised jeans and sweaters again for both of them and for Jo a chunky navy fleece with a hood in case it was chilly later on. Jo spent the morning making more cakes for Jack and, once these were iced and carefully packed in a plastic box, she begged to take off for Mill House.

'Jack won't mind if we're a bit early, will he?'

'You just want to see Bran,' accused Kate, laughing.

'True.' Jo's eyes danced. 'But you want to see Jack!'

When Kate turned down the drive to Mill House Jo's eyes were like saucers.

'Gosh, you were right,' she breathed in awe. 'It is a big garden.' She bit her lip, frowning.

'What's up now?'

Jo's knuckles were white as she gripped the box of cakes. 'If Jack is this rich I can't give him cakes as a present.'

'I can assure you,' said Kate with conviction, 'that he would like nothing better. Anyone can go out and buy something—like me. But you made him something with your own fair hands. Mega Brownie points for that, believe me.'

Jo relaxed, then said 'Wow!' as the house came into view. 'What a place—oh, and look, there's Mr Logan with Bran.' She put the box on the floor and was out of the car almost before Kate switched off the ignition. 'Hi, Mr Logan, hello Bran.'

Tom helped Kate from the car, smiling as he watched his granddaughter frolicking with the excited dog. 'How are you, my love?'

'As well as can be expected,' she said wryly, kissing him, then smiled radiantly as Jack came out of the house, a look in his eyes that warmed her right down to her toes. 'Good morning. How are you?'

'All the better for seeing you,' he assured her, and put his arm round her as he kissed her.

Joanna abandoned the dog to run to him. 'Hello, Jack. Happy Easter.'

'Likewise. Do I get a kiss too?'

Joanna promptly obliged, then turned to Tom Logan and reached up to kiss his cheek. 'Happy Easter, Mr Logan.'

'And a Happy Easter to you, sweetheart,' he said, clearing his throat. 'Let's go inside. Molly wants to meet you. It's all right, Jo,' he added, eyes twinkling. 'Bran can come too.'

'I've got to get something from the car first,' she said and ran to get her box of cakes. 'It's a little Easter present for you, Jack,' she said diffidently, taking off the lid.

He stood very still for a moment as he saw the cakes. Then he handed the box to his father and hugged Jo close. 'Thank you, pet. That's the nicest present I've ever had.'

'It certainly puts mine in the shade,' said Kate, resigned, and handed him one of the carrier bags she took out of the car. 'I've got one for you too, Tom.'

There was much laughter as the men received large chocolate Easter eggs with *Tom* written on one in white icing, and *Jack* on the other.

'But you have to share with me,' warned Kate. 'I love chocolate.'

'She certainly does,' said Jo as they went into the house. 'Kate ate more than half the box you gave me, Jack.'

'It's amazing she stays so slim,' he said, shaking his head, and smiled as he went into the kitchen. 'Molly, you've met Kate of course, but this is Joanna.'

'Hello, Miss Durant.' Molly wiped her hand on her apron and held it out, smiling. 'Hi, Joanna. I hear you went to a party last night. Did you have a good time?'

'I certainly did. Nice to meet you, Molly.' Jo shook the hand and sniffed the air. 'Wow! Something smells wonderful.'

'I hope you like turkey.' Molly turned to Kate. 'I've laid the table in here because the boss said it would be easier for you. Everything's ready. The turkey's in the warming oven with the vegetables, but the gravy should be heated through before you dish up.'

Kate handed her a carrier bag. 'Thank you, Molly. This is for you—just a little joke present to mark the occasion.'

The girl flushed with pleasure, stammering her thanks as

she received a chocolate egg inscribed *Molly* and, after instructions about ice cream in the freezer and a plate of treats for Bran in the refrigerator, the young cook wished them all a happy day and went home to her family.

'I'll show you the rest of the house after lunch, Jo,' said Jack, 'but I think we'd better eat now if the meal's ready.'

'You pour the wine, and I'll carve,' said his father, as Kate turned the heat up under the gravy. He took the turkey from the warming oven and put it on the table, then handed the oven gloves to Joanna. 'You can put the vegetable dishes on the table, love.'

Kate had been utterly convinced beforehand that she wouldn't be able to eat a thing, but in Jack's large, welcoming kitchen, with Jo so obviously enjoying herself, she relaxed and tucked into turkey and stuffing and roast potatoes with as much gusto as her child, who obviously considered Bran's presence in his bed the crowning touch to the meal.

'So tell us about the party,' said Jack, when Jo was into a second helping.

'It was just brilliant! In London I always felt like the odd one out at neighbours' parties because I'm away at school. But Josh and Leo made sure I knew everyone right from the start and they were all friendly so I had a really good time.'

'Did you dance a lot?' asked Tom.

'They don't dance, Dad,' teased Jack. 'They just prance around together.'

'We do dance,' said Jo indignantly, and smiled at him sweetly. 'It's just different from the minuets and things they did in your day.'

'*Touché*,' chuckled Tom Logan as Jack threw back his head and laughed, utterly delighted with his daughter.

'Cheeky!' said Kate, grinning.

'Josh and Leo asked if I could go to the cinema with them on Tuesday,' announced Jo, with a sideways look at Kate.

'Mrs Carey will bring them in and their dad will collect them from Park Crescent afterwards. If that's all right with you?'

Not daring to meet Jack's eyes, Kate agreed that it would be perfectly all right.

'Thanks, Kate. I met lots of people last night but I like Josh and Leo best,' added Jo. 'Because they're adopted, like me, I suppose. Did you know Mrs Carey was a twin?' she asked Jack.

'No—no, I didn't,' he said, and swallowed the rest of his wine.

'They prefer one of the parents to be a twin if they want to adopt twins,' Joanna informed the company at large.

Kate exchanged a wild look with Jack. 'When did Elizabeth tell you that you were adopted, Jo?'

'A long time ago, when I was in nursery school. She said other mothers had to take whatever baby God gave them, but she'd chosen me because I was special.' Joanna eyed her in surprise. 'You must have known about it.'

'Yes,' managed Kate. 'I knew. But Elizabeth never mentioned that she'd told you.'

Tom Logan shifted uneasily in his seat, and Kate smiled at him reassuringly. 'You look tired.'

'I didn't sleep much last night. Overdid the golf again,' he said unconvincingly.

'Jo didn't sleep enough last night, either,' said Kate as she got up to clear away plates. 'She found me walking in my sleep, so we had tea and hot chocolate in the middle of the night to recover.'

'It was all right,' said Jo, picking up a vegetable dish. 'Mummy told me that Kate did that sometimes, so I knew what was happening.'

'Pretty scary for you, just the same,' said Jack, meeting Kate's eyes.

'I've got something for you, Joanna,' said Tom, getting up. 'Come with me—yes, Bran, you can come too.'

Jo went with him eagerly, the dog padding after her, and Jack got up and caught Kate to him.

'I'll send Dad home and then we sit down with Jo. If she knows she's adopted she might as well know the rest of it.'

Kate put her head on his shoulder. 'You're right. I'll just load the dishwasher and clear up, then maybe we can walk in the garden. It might be easier outside.'

'It won't be easy anywhere,' said Jack heavily, 'but it has to be done.'

Between them they managed to make the kitchen tidy by the time Jo came back with Tom, carrying a huge Easter egg. She put it on the table and went straight to Kate to throw her arms round her, burrowing her face into her shoulder.

'I showed Joanna some photographs,' said Tom, his eyes meeting his son's. 'But I left the explanations to you.'

'*Dad*—' began Jack wrathfully, but Kate shook her head.

'I'm glad you did, Tom.' She put Jo away from her and looked into the dazed elfin face searchingly. 'Jack and I need to tell you a story, darling, to explain why you look just like the girl in the photograph.' Kate looked up. 'You needn't stay, Tom.'

'I started it, so of course I'll stay.'

'Then let's take Bran out into the garden,' suggested Jack. 'We'll make our confessions in the sunshine.'

'Confessions?' said Jo fearfully, looking from his face to Kate's.

Once outside the four of them paced along the gravel paths and around the millpond while Kate told Joanna her story. When she came to the part where she heard that Jack had married someone else, he took over and told his daughter how he'd been a fool to even look at another woman, let alone get into a situation where he felt he had to marry her.

'But you had to take responsibility for the baby,' said Jo, going straight to the heart of the matter.

'Exactly. But not only was the baby born too soon to survive, it turned out that I couldn't have been the father, so Dawn agreed to a divorce.'

'But what happened to your baby, Kate?' asked Jo. Then, seeing the look in Kate's eyes, she breathed in sharply, an incredulous look dawning in her own. 'Oh. You mean—' She swallowed hard. 'I'm the baby?'

'Yes, darling. Elizabeth persuaded me to let her bring you up because I was on my own and was quite ill for a while after you were born. Also I had to work and she could look after you better than I could.' Kate took in a deep, shaky breath. 'But it broke my heart to part with you.'

'And you look like the girl in the photograph because she's my mother,' said Jack with such obvious difficulty that Jo's lip trembled in sympathy. 'I've only just found out that I have the incredible luck to have a daughter, but Kate couldn't bear to tell you the truth because you're still grieving for the only parents you ever knew.'

Joanna stopped by a carved stone bench. 'I need to sit down.'

'Me, too,' said Tom, and took her hand to draw her down beside him.

Joanna fondled Bran as she looked up at Kate and Jack, who were leaning against each other for support. 'You know, I was going to look for my real mother one day, as long as you didn't mind, Kate.'

'Now you don't have to,' said her grandfather.

'No, I don't.' Jo was silent for a long time, but at last she stood up and flung her arms round Kate. 'Now I know why I've always felt so close to you. But I used to try and hide it so Mum wouldn't be hurt.'

'And I tried my best just to be Auntie,' said Kate unsteadily, 'but it was so *hard*. I could hardly bear it sometimes. I hated it when they sent you away to school. The day they took you off to Manor House I cried my eyes out.'

Jack had been very silent during this exchange, but Kate

could feel the tension in his body. She was about to put him out of his misery and ask Joanna how she felt about him when her child detached herself and held out her hand to him.

'I've only just met you so this is pretty weird.' She smiled shakily. 'But I'm sure I'll get used to you as my father pretty quickly now I know.'

'If this was a film,' said Kate, trying to introduce a lighter note into the situation since Jack was near to tears as he grasped his daughter's hand, 'you would run into his arms and cry "Daddy!"'

To her relief Jo chuckled. 'You've been watching too many TV movies.'

'I'd like it very much, just the same,' said Jack huskily.

'OK then,' said Jo, smiling at him, and stood on tiptoe to kiss his cheek as he put his arms round her and hugged her close. 'So what do I call you now?' she asked.

'Jack works for me,' he said promptly.

Jo nodded. 'Me, too.' She turned to Kate questioningly.

'I'm still the same old Kate, darling.'

'But I,' said Tom Logan, getting up from his seat, 'will only answer to Grandpa. OK?'

'OK,' agreed Jo, looked dazed. 'Gosh, this is all a lot to take in.'

'Let's go inside,' said Jack. 'Bran needs his dinner.'

'And I need some tea,' said Kate, suddenly weak at the knees from excess of emotion. 'While I enjoy a cup or two with Grandpa in front of the fire, perhaps you'd like to show Jo round the house, Jack.'

He assured her he was only too delighted and, after Jo had the pleasure of giving Bran his meal she went off with Jack. Kate watched them go with eyes which suddenly filled with tears. Tom Logan put his arms round her.

'There, there, darling, no need to cry. I was quite right, you know. Joanna is a mature enough child to understand.'

'And to forgive?'

'She doesn't see any need for forgiveness, Kate.'

Kate drew away to blow her nose and smiled up at him, comforted. 'I hope you're right.'

'Of course I am. Now, you make the tea and I'll carry the tray.'

When Jack and Joanna joined them in the living room Tom Logan smiled at them.

'Sorry, but I couldn't wait for you; I started on the cakes.'

'Then I'd better get stuck in before they vanish,' said Jack, filling a plate.

'What did you think of the house, Jo?' asked Kate.

Jo looked up from stroking Bran. 'It's fantastic. Jack said he did it all himself.'

'I had some help,' he admitted, grinning, and sat down by Kate. 'But the concept, the design and the interior décor is all my own work. I used to haunt the place while it was being restored. Some of the brickies and carpenters thought I was a pain in the neck.'

'But you had to see it was done properly,' said Jo in approval. 'Just like Kate and her house.'

Jack nodded. 'Talking of which, Jo, I think you ought to know that I want to marry Kate as soon as possible.'

'I have to agree because I've already turned him down twice,' Kate explained. 'He might never ask me again.' She smiled at Jo. 'Are you going to congratulate us?'

'Pretty weird, congratulating my own parents!' Jo smiled and bent to kiss Kate and Jack in turn. 'But I do—' She frowned suddenly. 'Does this mean you're going to sell your house, Kate, and come to live here?'

'Close,' said Kate. 'We're both coming to live here, if that's all right with you, Jo, and I'm going to make Aunt Edith's house over to you. If you're agreeable we'll let it out and you can have the rent money for your college fund. Do you want some tea?'

'No, thanks,' said Jo, stunned, and looked at Jack. 'Do you have a Coke or something?'

'Molly stocked me up, so I'm sure she thought of it. Go and forage in the kitchen, help yourself.'

'I'll come with you, Jo,' said Tom, and laughed. 'Look, Bran's coming too. You've made a hit there, love.'

When they were alone Kate turned to Jack anxiously. 'How do you feel?'

'Fantastic.' He let out a deep breath. 'I just want to sit here with you and fall apart with relief. She took it so well, didn't she?'

'Amazingly well.'

Jack rubbed his cheek against her hair. 'How do you think she'll react if I suggest adopting her officially?'

'I've no idea. If she wants to stay Joanna Sutton, you may have to live with that.'

'I can do it. At this moment in time I can do anything,' he said, and turned her face up to his to kiss her.

'Oops, don't look, Bran!' said Joanna, interrupting them. 'Be careful, Grandpa,' she warned, turning to Tom. 'Make sure you knock on doors from now on.'

He laughed and ruffled her hair. 'I had plenty of practice at that when they were young, believe me!'

'Right,' said Jack, getting up. 'Now we are all present again I have a certain omission to make good. Everyone received a present today except Kate.' He took a box from his pocket and went down on one knee in front of her. 'Here we go again. For the third time of asking, Katherine Margaret Durant, will you be my wife?'

'Oh, yes, please,' she said, so fervently Joanna giggled.

'Don't try to give it back again,' said Jack sternly as he slid his mother's ring on Kate's finger.

'No chance,' she assured him and waggled her fingers at Jo as she bent to examine the ring. 'This belonged to your grandmother—the girl in the photograph.'

'It's so pretty! I don't know how you could bear to part with it last time,' said Jo, examining the posy of diamonds, and smiled at Jack. 'My name's Margaret, too.'

His eyes flew to Kate who nodded. 'I told you I laid down the law about the names. So she is Joanna, which is the nearest I could get to your baptismal name of John, and Margaret after your mother.'

Seeing that his son was momentarily deprived of words, Tom Logan blew his nose loudly. 'Right then. Now Joanna knows the truth, when are you two going to tie the knot?'

'I hadn't thought that far,' said Kate, eying her daughter uneasily.

'I had,' said Jack with feeling.

'If you get a special licence,' said Jo matter-of-factly, 'you could get married just before I go back to school, then you wouldn't have to worry about me while you were away on your honeymoon.' She grinned broadly as her parents stared at her open-mouthed. 'You're not getting any younger, so why hang about?'

'My sentiments exactly,' said her grandfather in approval.

'Besides, Bran and I want to be bridesmaids,' said Jo, hugging the dog.

On a sunny, brisk April day there was a big turnout for the marriage of John Logan to Katherine Durant. Due to the hole-and-corner misery of his first marriage, Jack had insisted on celebrating in style as he finally married the love of his life. Miss Joanna Sutton, soon to be officially Joanna Logan, was chief bridesmaid, Mrs Ben Maitland having regretfully declined the office of matron of honour due to her rapidly increasing girth.

Tall and elegant in formal morning coat, Jack turned at the altar with Ben Maitland as the organist began the wedding march, and smiled, a lump in his throat, as he saw his bride, in a narrow dress of champagne slipper satin, enter the church on his father's arm, with their daughter close behind in a matching chiffon which, she told Anna, made her look like the fairy off the Christmas tree, but which secretly was exactly the kind of dress she'd always yearned for. She winked at the Carey twins as she passed and beamed at Anna. But when she smiled reassuringly at her father as she took the bride's bouquet, Jack smiled back so proudly she felt warm inside.

The sun shone on the wedding group as the photographers dodged about, with much laughter from the assembled guests when the bridesmaid insisted on the inclusion of a handsome black retriever in all the shots, complete with brand-new leash and a rose thrust through his collar. The reception in the hall of Mill House was a very animated affair with an array of Molly's delicious food that had all the guests demanding the name of the caterer, and after Ben had made a witty, entertaining speech and proposed the health of the enchanting bridesmaid and her canine escort, Jack waited for silence, then smiled down at his wife and across the hall at the daughter standing between the Carey twins with Bran.

'Today I've finally been united with the beautiful woman I wanted to marry years ago, the moment I first set eyes on her. And, to add to my incredible good fortune in doing so, I also gained a beautiful daughter.'

'Logan's luck,' shouted someone, above the applause. The Carey twins cheered as Jack beckoned Joanna over to stand beside him and he grinned at them, then kissed Kate and Jo in turn and raised his glass. 'Ladies and gentlemen, please join me in a toast to Kate and Joanna, for making me the happiest—*and* luckiest—man on the planet.'

REQUEST YOUR FREE BOOKS!

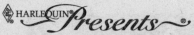 HARLEQUIN® *Presents*~

 PASSION GUARANTEED SEDUCTION

2 FREE NOVELS PLUS 2 FREE GIFTS!

YES! Please send me 2 FREE Harlequin Presents® novels and my 2 FREE gifts. After receiving them, if I don't wish to receive any more books, I can return the shipping statement marked "cancel." If I don't cancel, I will receive 6 brand-new novels every month and be billed just $3.80 per book in the U.S., or $4.47 per book in Canada, plus 25¢ shipping and handling per book and applicable taxes, if any*. That's a savings of close to 15% off the cover price! I understand that accepting the 2 free books and gifts places me under no obligation to buy anything. I can always return a shipment and cancel at any time. Even if I never buy another book from Harlequin, the two free books and gifts are mine to keep forever.

106 HDN EEXK 306 HDN EEXV

Name	(PLEASE PRINT)	
Address		Apt. #
City	State/Prov.	Zip/Postal Code

Signature (if under 18, a parent or guardian must sign)

Mail to the **Harlequin Reader Service®**:
IN U.S.A.: P.O. Box 1867, Buffalo, NY 14240-1867
IN CANADA: P.O. Box 609, Fort Erie, Ontario L2A 5X3

Not valid to current Harlequin Presents subscribers.

**Want to try two free books from another line?
Call 1-800-873-8635 or visit www.morefreebooks.com.**

* Terms and prices subject to change without notice. NY residents add applicable sales tax. Canadian residents will be charged applicable provincial taxes and GST. This offer is limited to one order per household. All orders subject to approval. Credit or debit balances in a customer's account(s) may be offset by any other outstanding balance owed by or to the customer. Please allow 4 to 6 weeks for delivery.

Your Privacy: Harlequin is committed to protecting your privacy. Our Privacy Policy is available online at www.eHarlequin.com or upon request from the Reader Service. From time to time we make our lists of customers available to reputable firms who may have a product or service of interest to you. If you would prefer we not share your name and address, please check here. ☐

HP07

Wined, dined and swept away by a British billionaire!

Don't be late!

He's suave and sophisticated.
He's undeniably charming.
And above all, he treats her like a lady.

But don't be fooled....

Beneath the tux, there's a primal passionate lover
who's determined to make her his!

Gabriella is in love with wealthy Rufus Gresham,
but he believes she's a gold digger.
Then they are forced to marry.... Will Rufus use
this as an excuse to get Gabriella in his bed?

Another British billionaire is coming your way in May 2007.

WIFE BY CONTRACT, MISTRESS BY DEMAND
by Carole Mortimer

Book #2633

www.eHarlequin.com   HPDAE0507

**From the magnificent Blue Palace to the wild
plains of the desert, be swept away as three
sheikh princes find their brides.**

When English girl Sorrel announces she wishes to
explore the pleasures of the West, Sheikh Malik
must take action—if she wants to learn the ways
of seduction, he will be the one to teach her....

THE DESERT KING'S
VIRGIN BRIDE
by Sharon Kendrick

Book #2628

Coming in May 2007.